BREAK ME

A SHATTERED SERIES NOVEL

J.M. WALKER

Cover Design and Formatting: Just write. Creations

IBSN: 978-0-9938369-8-5

DEDICATION

To my husband Michael. Without you, none of this would be possible.

ACKNOWLEDGEMENTS

First off I would like to thank everyone who has helped me with this unexpected journey and dream of mine. You all know who you are and without your support, this wouldn't have happened for me.

Thank you to my friends and family for your love and constant encouragement. Sometimes a girl needs a little coddling.

Thank you to Chrissy (C.A. Szarek) for EVERYTHING! Bestie, you are my inspiration, and words cannot express how much I am grateful for all you have done for me.

To my sister, Shawna…you are my rock. Thank you for telling me to "just write."

My beta readers: You ladies are a solid source of helpfulness and you definitely don't have any qualms about telling me when I really screwed up my grammar or storyline. Love you girlies!

To my girls who helped me swear!!! Who would have thought I needed help in that department with all the movies I've watched and books I've read? So thank you!

To my girls at my review blog, Twinsie Talk Book Reviews; Angie, Brenda, Melinda, Jen, Kristi and Deb, thank you for everything. I love you like sisters!

To my online book club (you know who you are) and my coworkers. Thank you for constantly putting up with all of my book talk and rants and raves about my characters being difficult.

To my readers. Thank you. I love you and I can't do this without you.

xx

CHAPTER ONE

HE'S HERE.

As I walked to the same seat at the same window that I had been sitting at each morning for the last month, I felt him watching me. My body warmed, and when I sat down, I looked up. Dark eyes gazed at me, caressing me with just a look. It was the first time he had noticed me, and it made my stomach flip.

The coffee shop buzzed with activity, distracting me enough to turn away from his heated stare.

My gaze flicked back to his, and a hint of disappointment settled in my belly when he was no longer looking at me.

I couldn't help but stare as he leaned back in his chair, newspaper in hand, and brought his coffee up to full, kissable lips.

A black leather jacket just waiting to be pulled off of him covered his large frame that showcased power and domination. Images of me ripping off his black T-shirt flew through my mind. Wow…no man has ever made me think thoughts like these.

His V-neck T-shirt showed a hint of tattoos covering his torso with thick arms that I would love to feel wrapped around me. He definitely looked like a man who got what he wanted, when he wanted it.

I always overheard the baristas joking around about who he was, but no one actually knew him. Not having the courage to actually go up to him myself, I waited to see if he would come to me, and he didn't. Not yet anyway.

His gaze flashed up to mine, interrupting my thoughts, and my cheeks heated at being caught staring at him. A small smirk tugged at the corner of his lips before he stood from his seat.

I quickly looked down and pulled my book out of my bag, opening it to the bookmarked page. Clearing my throat, I ignored the rapid beating of my heart. Oh God, he's coming over here.

A moment later, the chair across from me squeaked as it was dragged across the floor.

The scent of fresh laundry, soap, and man filled my nostrils, making my heart pitter-patter at the intoxicating smell.

I looked up into a set of deep, warm brown eyes surrounded by long lashes that would make any girl envious. He was simply breathtaking, and the hint of a smile on his lips showed that he knew he was getting to me.

His short black hair shouted that running his fingers through it was about all the styling he went for. A five o'clock shadow covered his jawline that somehow made him look scarier and sexier. He grabbed the book out of my hand and leaned back in his chair, flipping through the pages.

I frowned. "Excuse me?"

He looked at me and raised an eyebrow. "Is there a problem?" His voice was deep and smooth like silk.

Ignoring the way it made my heart flutter, I rolled my eyes. "No, of course not. Now why would there be a problem? You only snatched my book out of my hand while I was trying to read it but no, no problem."

His lips turned up at the corners and then tapped the cover of my book. "I think you were checking me out more than you were reading."

I gaped at his brutal honesty. Sexy confidence oozed off of him, and all I could do was stare. Not having any witty comeback, I crossed my arms under my chest.

"I never pictured you as the romance-reading type," he added.

"And what's wrong with reading romance?" I asked.

Black eyes narrowed at me. "It usually means you can't get a piece in real life, so you have to resort to masturbating to paper or porn, but…" He lifted my book, "Looking at this cover, it looks like it could be a bit of both."

I scoffed. "Please. Maybe in some cases that may be true, but I'm sure a lot of women enjoy the actual storylines. I, for one, just read it for entertainment."

"Yeah, I don't think you'd have any issues getting a piece in real life." His voice became sensual as his gaze lowered to my mouth and down, stopping at my chest. He smirked.

Tingles washed over my skin at his heated stare. My throat dried up instantly as the current in the room shifted.

He was sex on a stick, and he was flirting with me, making my stomach jump with glee.

Clearing his throat, he bit back a laugh.

"What?" I asked, confused, looking down. No coffee had slopped on me, so I was good as far as that went.

"Oh, nothing." He massaged his chin, rubbing his fingers along the scruff of his jaw.

My gaze instantly went to his lips, and I wondered what it would be like to kiss him. Shaking that thought out of my head, I leaned forward. He clearly was not a man of many words. "You were going to say something."

He smiled and continued flipping through the pages of my book. "No, I wasn't."

I huffed, drumming my fingers on the table. I so did not have patience for him or his crap. "Seriously, what were you going to say?"

Leaning forward, his gaze flicked to mine and then down to my mouth, a small smile forming on his lips. "I was going to ask you how far down that blush went."

My mouth parted, and my heart thudded against my chest.

His gaze flicked back up to mine, and he chuckled, sitting back in his chair.

Ass. "Are you done?"

He flipped through a couple of more pages and stopped, his eyes moving back and forth along the page.

"Are you seriously reading my…"

He held up his hand, stopping me.

I rolled my head back, and sighed dramatically.

"Did you guys need anything else?"

My head snapped up, and I saw a barista standing in front of me. Focusing on her nametag, I politely smiled. "No thank you, Brenda."

She nodded in response and walked away, her graying bob bouncing against her shoulders.

Turning back to my new friend, I sighed loudly again and tapped my fingers on the table.

"Wow, this is some good shit right here. I should take notes," he said, reaching into his coat.

My mouth dropped open. Did this guy actually think that he had issues in getting a woman? Or man, depending on what he went for. "Are you serious?"

He looked up at me, his lips set in a straight line, no emotion on his face whatsoever. "What?"

"Really? Really. You think you should take notes? Seriously?" This guy was nuts.

He didn't respond, and then a moment later, a huge grin broke out on his face. "Well, I thought it sounded good."

I shook my head and chuckled at his poor attempt at being funny.

He laughed and gave me back my book.

Something about him made me feel comfortable enough that I could be myself around him. I didn't have to pretend to be something I wasn't, unlike with other men.

A moment later, he stopped laughing, a small smile still curving his lips. "I love your laugh."

My gaze snapped to his and my cheeks warmed. One compliment from him and I was mush. Putty in his hands. Oh, crap. "Thank you," I said quietly.

His eyes blazed, and my heart beat loudly against my chest. I cleared my throat and put my book away, needing the distraction.

"You want another coffee?" he asked a moment later.

I looked up, and he motioned to my empty coffee mug. "Sure, please."

Giving him my order, I watched as he headed to the counter. He leaned against it, talking to the barista and looked back at me. The barista said something funny, and he laughed, still keeping his gaze locked with mine.

My skin tingled as his stare roamed over me. His dark eyes instantly had that effect on me. Like he was searching into my soul for all my deepest, darkest secrets.

He looked away when the barista came back with our drinks.

I turned back to the table and frowned. Where the hell was my phone?

Searching through my bag, I came up empty-handed. I huffed, trying to remember if I had even brought my phone with me in the first place.

"What are you looking for?" he asked as he neared the table. Placing the drinks in between us, he sat down.

As an afterthought, I thanked him for the coffee. "I can't seem to find my phone."

"Hmm…maybe it's in your purse."

"Maybe." I reached down for my bag and searched through it again. My eyes widened when my fingers wrapped around something hard and rectangular.

I pulled out my cell phone and frowned. I was confused as to why I couldn't find it just a moment ago. "I swear it wasn't there."

He shrugged and took a sip of his coffee. "So, what's your name, little one?"

My face warmed at his term of endearment. "Tori McLeod."

"Well, it's nice to meet you, Tori." He stuck out his hand.

The way he said my name, it came out low and deep, and it sent shivers down my spine.

Placing my hand in his, electricity ran down my spine as soon as we made contact. I swallowed. "Nice to meet you too…"

"Sebastian Chelios, but you can call me whatever you damn well please." He smirked.

I scoffed. "Does that sort of pickup line work on every girl, or is this your first time testing it out?"

He chuckled. "Well, that depends."

My eyebrow rose. "On?"

His gaze darkened, and he placed a kiss on my knuckles. "Is it working?"

I opened my mouth to speak, but no words formed on my tongue as I watched his lips brush over the back of my hand.

He chuckled harder and leaned back in his seat.

I huffed and took a final sip of my coffee. Packing up my things, I rose from the chair. "I should go."

Sebastian shoved back his chair and rose. He looked down at me, our bodies mere inches from each other. "It was really nice meeting you, little one."

"You too," I said quietly.

His hand reached out and tucked a strand of my hair behind my ear, causing my heart to pitter-patter.

Images of our bodies entwined together, writhing and moving as one, flashed in my mind. My face grew hot.

"I'll see you later, Tori."

Nodding, I flung my bag over my shoulder and headed to the door. Pausing, I looked back at Sebastian. He wasn't at the table. My eyes did a quick scan of the coffee shop, and I didn't see him anywhere.

I sighed and pushed the door open, frowning at the gloomy weather. A cool draft washed over me, sending shivers down my spine.

Heading home, I walked the five blocks, like I did all the time, while scrolling through the music list on my phone.

Suddenly, a rough hand grabbed my arm, yanked me into a dark nearby alley and covered my mouth before I could scream.

My heart sped up, and I broke out in a cold sweat.

Oh God. This is it. I'm going to be raped.

My bag fell from my hands.

The ear buds were yanked from my ears, and my attacker growled, pushing me face-first against the brick wall of the building.

"Please. Just take my purse. Take my money, just please don't hurt me." Tears welled in my eyes, and I squeezed them shut as my heart thudded loudly against my chest.

"I'm not going to hurt you, little one," my attacker whispered.

Sebastian.

My stomach dropped, anger replacing fear. I slowly opened my eyes. "Sebastian! What the hell do you think you're doing?"

Before I got a response, I felt his hard body lean into mine, and I gasped as his erection pressed against my ass. Well, that was unexpected. I had no idea that he wanted me as badly as I wanted him. He was arrogant as all get out, and yet his body seemed to have a mind of its own as well.

"Sebastian," I said, breathless, the bulge in his jeans indicating that he was definitely not small, and as he ground his hips against me, I had more than a feeling that he knew how to use it.

He spun me around, lowering his mouth to mine. His breath was hot on my lips as I looked up into his eyes. Placing my hands on his broad shoulders, I watched as hunger and desire swam through his dark gaze. His lips parted, and a pink tongue slipped out, licking them.

Warm shivers spread throughout my body at the sight.

Wrapping a hand around my neck, he smirked before slamming his mouth down on mine, the rough impact making my lips tingle.

I kissed him back, and the feel of his hard lower body against my pelvis ignited a passion in me that I hadn't felt in a very long time.

He pressed his body against me, pushing me up against the wall. The rough stubble of his jaw scratched at my cheeks. His hot tongue forced its way between my lips, sucking and pulling as he went.

I moaned as he slowed the movements that shot tingles to my groin. My body instantly responded to his touch, nipples peaking at the feel of the hard body surrounding me.

His hands went to my hips then to my ass, squeezing, pulling me closer to him. It wasn't enough. I needed him in me. No man had ever made me feel that way with just a kiss. He ground his lower body into mine, and I whimpered against his mouth.

My hands went up around his neck of their own accord. I curled my fingers through his soft hair, lightly tugging. I deepened the kiss, causing a groan to come from his chest. The guttural sound vibrated through my bones, sending shivers up and down my spine.

Out of nowhere, he released my mouth, his chest rising and falling with ragged breaths.

"I needed to know." His voice was raspy as the pad of his thumb ran over my bottom lip before he placed a soft kiss on my swollen lips.

I frowned, confused. "Know what?" I panted, gripping his shirt in my hand.

"If your lips tasted as good as they looked."

Heat spread through my body at his words, and ignoring the sounds of the city around us, I reached my fingers under his shirt, grazing the soft skin of his hard waist. "And?"

He lightly chuckled and kissed the corner of my mouth, grinding his hips against mine. "Do I really need to answer that, little one?"

"Mmm...I guess not." I was dying to see him naked. To see all of his tattoos. To kiss the hard contours of his no-doubt insanely hard abs.

He trailed kisses along my jawline and down my neck. His other hand moved back to my ass and pulled me flush against him. "God, you fucking smell good."

I closed my eyes and moaned, squeezing his arms.

"But the only thing better for those gorgeous plump lips of yours..." He licked up the side of my neck.

"…would be…" His mouth closed over the bottom of my ear, and a sharp pain shot pleasure straight to my groin.

I whimpered.

"…if they were wrapped…" He kissed the sensitive spot just under my ear.

Oh God.

"…around my…"

My eyes popped open and my loins quivered at his words. "Sebastian."

He smirked and placed one last kiss on my mouth. Putting my ear buds back in my ears, he took a step back, his gaze boring into mine. A hint of mischief danced around in them as he turned and walked out of the alley.

CHAPTER TWO

WELL, THAT WAS A new experience for me.

After the shock of what had happened in the alley wore off, I really regretted not giving him my number. As much as I was not a fan of one-night stands, to have him in my bed—or anywhere, for that matter—would definitely please the ache that had now formed in my belly. Or, now that I thought of it, it would probably just make it worse.

I've had my fair share of sexual experiences, but nothing compared to what Sebastian did to me. One look from him and it's like I melted into a pile of girlie goo. I should have been ashamed of myself, but I ached for him, and a part of me hoped he felt the same way about me.

After my encounter with him, I didn't see him in the coffee shop again for the rest of the week.

I spent that time searching for a job, but had no such luck.

The baristas would always giggle and whisper when I came in, as if they knew something that I didn't. Did they know about my alley adventure? Oh God. I didn't see any cameras, but what if a stranger had walked by and saw us?

A week and a half later, I walked into the coffee shop and hoped to see him there sitting at his usual table. When I didn't see him, a flutter of disappointment settled in my belly.

Every time I thought of Sebastian, my body grew inflamed. He was like a drug, and I needed my fix. I was addicted to him already. He was dark and brooding, and unable to control myself, I was drawn to him.

I was sitting at my usual spot in the little coffee shop, reading, when a dark shadow covered my page.

A masculine scent filled my nostrils, and before looking up, I knew exactly who it was. My body hummed as if it recognized him.

The same intoxicating smell of fresh soap and man forced its way into my nose much like the owner had forced his way into my life.

I took a deep breath and lifted my eyes. Seeing him sit across from me set my body on overdrive with the anticipation of being touched by him again.

Something about this man made me want him. I craved him, even though instinctively I knew he was dangerous.

Ever since the first time I saw him and our subsequent encounter in the alley, I couldn't get him out of my head. The feel of his lips on mine, his hard body pressed up against me, pushing me into the wall. I wanted him. I needed him, and that sent a nervous flutter racing through my stomach. No man had ever had this much impact on me with just two encounters.

My heart thudded against my rib cage, and my cheeks grew hot under his intense gaze.

"Hello, little one." His deep, smooth voice washed over my skin like melted chocolate, making my mouth water.

Images of our moment in the alley and what he'd said to me popped into my head. I swallowed hard. "Hello, Sebastian."

He was wearing the same black leather jacket over a white cotton shirt this time, and his tattoos peeked out from the collar around his thick neck. What I wouldn't give to see how far down under his shirt those tattoos went.

"So, how've you been?" he asked casually.

"Hmm?"

Did he ask me a question?

A grin spread on his face. "I asked, how have you been?"

"Oh…" My skin heated. "I've been…um…good."

A smug smile formed on his distractingly handsome face. "Something on your mind, little one?"

I coughed. I'd say. My gaze kept flicking back to his lips. Lips that had kissed me. I had it so bad for him. "You could say that. How have you been?"

"I've been good too. Very, very good." Lust danced in his gaze as he looked at my lips like he was also remembering our very heated kiss in the alley.

My skin heated. Oh God. What was it about him that had me practically begging at his feet?

"Now, why are you distracted, little one?" He was teasing me.

If he actually thought I was going to come out and say it, he had another think coming. I cleared my throat again. "No reason."

"I think you're lying, but that's fine. I'm sure I'll find out eventually." He casually leaned back in the chair, all the while not taking his gaze from mine.

My cheeks were red hot under his intense scrutiny. Taking a sip of my coffee, I ignored him. Or tried to, at least.

"I love making you blush." A hint of amusement coated his voice. He was definitely confident in his sexual abilities. He probably had reason to be. Tori, do not think about that right now.

I rolled my eyes. "I am not blushing."

His eyes darkened. "Really?"

My throat went dry, and I nodded. "I do not blush."

Sebastian laughed. "Well, we'll just have to change that."

I gasped when I felt a tug on my chair. He pulled me as close to the table as possible.

I was stuck. With the chair having arms on it and it being pulled tight to the edge, I couldn't back up or move it at all. I looked down on either side of me and saw his feet holding the chair legs.

Moving forward, he pointed at the book in my hands. "Still reading porn, I see."

I noticed the tattoos covered his hands as well. No wedding ring marked his left hand, and I breathed a sigh of relief. For some reason the thought of him being single made me giddy.

I raised an eyebrow. "Seriously? Is this how you get a girl's attention?"

"This…" His eyes blazed and he licked his lips. "And other ways."

My heart beat loudly against my chest, and tingles of anticipation at being kissed by him again coursing through my body. "Yeah, well, it helps pass the time while I look for a job."

"I can think of better ways to pass the time." His voice lowered suggestively.

I cleared my throat and shook that thought out of my head. "I bet you could, but since we're in a public place, that might not be a good idea."

He laughed. "You have a point. As much as I would love to be caught naked with you…"

The way he said naked sent shivers up my spine. Trying to be strong and resist his temptation, I tugged on my chair. "Let me go."

"I'll let you go soon." Then he took the book from me, pausing to draw tiny, tingly, circles on the back of my hand with his thumb. A moment later, he placed the book on the table. "Why are you reading this? It's probably boring as hell."

"Yeah, well, I'm sure it's better than anything you could come up with."

Filter, Tori, filter.

He raised an eyebrow, and an evil glint flashed through his eyes.

Oh, shit.

My eyes widened as he reached across and grabbed my wrist. His rough, calloused fingers gently smoothed over my pulse point. He brought my hand up to his mouth, and I watched as he kissed each one of my fingers while massaging my palm with his thumbs.

Each movement sent jolts of electricity straight to my groin; all the while he kept his eyes on me.

My mouth parted and my breathing picked up. I stared as he kissed his way down my fingers to the middle of my palm. When he reached the spot above my wrist, he opened his mouth, and I gasped when he lightly bit it, sending liquid pooling in my panties.

Oh God.

I didn't want him to stop. "Oh…my…" I said breathily.

A mischievous look flicked in his eyes as he kissed my wrist and gently placed it back on the table. He released my chair, stood up, and walked around behind me. His broad chest pressed into my back as he leaned down and placed his hands on either side of me.

I closed my eyes as the heat from his body seeped into mine. The light scent of soap and man filled my nostrils. It was intoxicating. Hot breath grazed my ear and my neck, sending shivers down my spine.

"You are definitely blushing now," he whispered, placing a kiss on my neck.

"Sebastian." My heart thumped against my chest, and I bit my bottom lip.

"What, little one?"

"I…I…" Words wouldn't form properly on my tongue.

He chuckled. "Is there something you want?"

Oh God.

He was going to make me say it, wasn't he? "Please…I…"

"Yes?"

Fuck it.

I leaned down and reached into my bag, pulling out a piece of paper and a pen. I quickly wrote down my address and phone number.

"Little one…"

I frowned as I heard the question in his voice asking me if I was sure. I was. "Take it. Before I change my mind," I whispered.

Sebastian grabbed the paper out of my hand. "I'll be seeing you soon, little one." His voice was husky. He placed another kiss on my neck that sent tremors of heat through my body.

I turned my head, watching him walk out of the coffee shop. My blood pounded hard in my ears at his unexpected promise. Taking a couple of deep breaths, I leaned back in my chair. What the hell did I just do?

CHAPTER THREE

I HAD GIVEN A complete and total stranger my address and phone number. Not being in the habit of sleeping with random men, I was nervous about the possibility of him showing up at my place unannounced.

My body reacted more quickly than my brain did, so while I was writing down my address and phone number, I ignored that little voice in my head that told me to stay away from him. Sebastian definitely was a man who knew what he wanted and when he wanted it, and I think even if I wanted to stay away from him, that would be near impossible.

No man had ever made my loins quiver just by kissing the palm of my hand. If he could do that with just a kiss, who knew what else he could do?

I looked up and saw one of the baristas headed toward me. She sat in the seat across from me. Tight brown curls framed her oval face, and she had the biggest bright green eyes I had ever seen.

"Girl, please tell me that you're sleeping with that man."

"Uh…"

"Because what I just saw was totally fucking hot." She fanned herself.

I leaned forward, placing an elbow on the table. "I only just met him…"

Her eyes widened. "Really? Well I hope it works out for you."

I just gave him my address and phone number. It had better work out. Feeling ashamed of myself, I smiled tightly. "Thank you."

She held her hand out in front of me. "My name's Keisha Lee. I work here pretty much every day, and if you sleep with him, I want details."

I laughed and shook her hand.

Keisha had a fiery, bubbly spirit about her, and when she smiled, it reached her eyes, lighting up her whole face. I liked her.

"I've seen you here a lot. We should hang out some time."

I also appreciated her forwardness. "Sure, that sounds fun."

"Awesome, and you are…"

"Oh, sorry. A little distracted. I'm Tori McLeod."

"It's understandable. Distracted by Mr. Bodacious. He's gorgeous." She waggled her eyebrows.

I giggled. "Yeah, he is." My skin warmed just thinking about him.

"Did you get his name?"

"Sebastian Chelios."

She gaped. "Wow, even his name is hot."

I laughed. "Yeah, it is."

"Well, it's nice to meet you, Tori." Her smile seemed to turn brighter at that thought.

We chatted for the rest of the night until the coffee shop closed, making plans for the next day to go shopping.

***

Over the next couple of weeks, Keisha and I hung out regularly, becoming friends. She told me about her brother owning a nightclub, so we decided to make an appearance. I hadn't heard from Sebastian, and even though I never truly expected him to call me or show up at my place, a part of me was disappointed. So, Keisha and I were going to go out and have a good time. Apparently I needed a night out anyway, according to her.

Showing up at the coffee shop with ten minutes to spare, I sat in my regular seat.

I'd settled on casual and comfortable, wearing dark blue skinny jeans and a white tank top. I'd drawn my long, straight black hair up in a ponytail and wore little make-up.

"Are you ready?" Keisha walked up to the table, sporting the casual uniform of the small café. Her eyes were bright and full of life. I envied her bubbly personality.

"Yes, I am." I smiled and stood.

"You're not wearing that, are you?"

I frowned and looked down at myself. "What's wrong with what I'm wearing?"

She rolled her eyes and grabbed my hand. "Come on."

We left the coffee shop and walked to the end of the street where Keisha hailed a cab. "I only live about two blocks away, but I don't want to wear out my dancing feet." She winked at me and opened the door to the cab when it pulled up. She slid over, and I followed in behind her.

Keisha gave the cab driver her address, and his eyebrow rose. "What? I don't want to wear myself out before the night begins, if you must know."

I laughed and she glared at me.

A moment later a giggle escaped her lips, and we were both in hysterics by the time we reached her apartment building.

Growing up, I'd never had a friend quite like Keisha. She was a spitball of fire, and in the short time that I'd known her, I could already see us becoming lifelong friends.

She was a little bit shorter than me, but her big personality made up for it.

When we reached her apartment, Keisha practically dove out of the vehicle after paying the cabbie.

Shaking my head, I smiled and followed her to the big brick building in front of us.

It was a three-story walk-up that was between a Chinese restaurant and a mini grocery store.

As we approached Keisha's apartment, I heard loud noises coming from behind a door down the hall. I laughed once I realized what was causing them.

She laughed along with me. "Sounds like they're having a good time."

"Yeah, no doubt." A wave of jealousy flowed through me, settling in the pit of my stomach.

Oh, what I wouldn't give for a night like that.

Hearing the woman scream and moan from the other apartment instantly made an image of Sebastian pop into my head.

I sighed. I so had it bad for him.

"You're thinking about him, aren't you?"

"What? Are you psychic or something?"

Keisha giggled. "No, I just know how to read people, and it's obvious 'cause you're blushing."

I huffed. "I swear, that man is the only damn one to ever make me blush, and it's very annoying."

"Oh Tor, you really need to get him out of your system."

I turned back toward Keisha. "Yeah, I do."

She laughed again and grabbed my hand, yanking me from my spot at the door. As she dragged me toward her bedroom, I noticed her cozy living room that was vibrant with color, just like its owner. It was my first time in her apartment since meeting her a couple of weeks ago but I could see that her style was very much like her personality.

"Keisha, I think I did something stupid." I'd never told her about giving Sebastian my address and phone number, and it was eating me up inside.

"Oh?"

"I gave him my address and phone number." I said quickly.

Her eyes widened. "You did what? I know I haven't known you for long but I feel I should say this anyway. Are you fucking crazy?"

My face heated. "Trust me, I was thinking the same thing."

"Girl…" She shook her head.

I followed Keisha as we walked down a narrow hall lined with picture frames that were empty. I was about to ask why they were still empty when she caught me looking at them.

"I haven't found anyone deserving enough to be in my frames except for my brother." She answered my question for me, pointing to a handsome man who was posing with her in one of the smaller frames.

"I like them."

"I liked them too, so I bought them all." She smiled at me. "Maybe you'll be in one of them someday."

I smiled back. "I think I would like that."

"Now back to the Sebastian thing… I can't really judge about you giving out your phone number and address to a guy you just met 'cause girlfriend, trust me, I probably would've done the exact same thing." She laughed and pulled me into her bedroom.

"Well that makes me feel somewhat…" My eyes went wide. There were clothes everywhere. On her bed, her desk, her dresser…it was like a clothing store threw up in her room.

"Um, Keisha…"

She looked back at me and noticed my reaction. "Don't mind the mess. I'm a bit of a slob."

Yeah, no kidding.

Keisha released my hand and walked to her closet. "Ok, now what can we get you to wear to make all the guys' eyes pop out of their heads?"

I crossed my arms under my chest and raised an eyebrow.

She turned back to me and sighed. "Fine, what can you wear to make Sebastian's eyes pop out of his head?"

"I don't think I have any issues in that department," I mumbled.

She laughed. "Yeah, probably not." She gave me a once-over. "Hmm…" Tapping her chin, she crossed her other arm under her chest. "Well, you are hot and you have a smoking body. Okay, will you change just one thing for me then?"

"Sure." I frowned.

"What size are your feet?" She looked down at my feet and scowled at my black flats.

"Eight," I said, following her gaze.

She clapped her hands together. "Perfect!" She turned around and started digging through the bottom of her closet. She threw stuff out behind her, and I actually had to dodge a couple of shoe boxes and clothing items so I wouldn't get hit in the head.

"I know they're here somewhere," she mumbled.

A few moments later, she rose and handed me a pair of black high heels that looked to be about four inches high.

She expects me to walk in these?

I looked down at the shoes in her hand. "Um…I don't think I could walk or even dance in these shoes."

She shoved them at me. "Try them on. You never know. There's a floor-length mirror on the back of the door."

Grabbing the shoes out of her hand, I walked to her door and closed it. I put the shoes on. They were hot. They made my legs look a mile long. I took a couple of steps to the left and then to the right, surprised at how easy they were to walk in.

"Um…Keisha?"

"Oh, my gosh. You look gorgeous, Tori! Those shoes are perfect."

Both of us were looking in the mirror at my feet.

"Thank you. I love them. I just hope I can dance in them."

Keisha shrugged her shoulders. "Just take them off if you have to. That's what I do, but I'm sure you'll be fine. Sebastian could always hold you up anyway if your feet get tired."

I rolled my eyes and laughed. "You say that like he's going to be at the club tonight."

"Well…" She turned and grabbed a dress from her closet and walked to the bathroom, shutting the door behind her.

"Well, what?"

"I've seen him at this club we're going to. He's a regular." Her voice was muffled by the closed door, so I waited for her to finish dressing.

A moment later, she re-entered her bedroom sporting a skin-tight black dress that hugged her curves.

"You look beautiful."

Keisha smiled, revealing a set of perfect white teeth. Her brown curls were piled on her head in a messy bun, and ringlets fell down, framing her lightly tanned face. Black kohl outlined her bright green eyes, and pale pink lipstick coated her full lips.

"And I love the dress."

"Oh, this old thing?" She winked.

I laughed, grabbing my clutch.

Turning around, she went back to her closet and pulled out a pair of red-satin pumps.

"Now, did you say that Sebastian is a regular at the club we're going to tonight?"

"Yes, I did."

My heart thudded in my chest at the thought of seeing him again so soon. "Oh…well…this could get interesting."

"Yes, it could. Just be careful."

"Yes, mother."

CHAPTER FOUR

SINCE MOVING TO THE city, college and looking for a job took up most of my time. Being on a scholarship, I had to work extra hard to maintain good grades, so I spent most of my days behind a book, studying.

Keisha was the first friend I had made since moving and I was determined to enjoy myself tonight.

After getting ready, we took a cab to The Red Love, the hottest new club in town, according to Keisha, anyway. She also exclaimed how hot the owner was but I think she only said that because she was related to him.

Loud music seeped from the doorway, and I already felt the beat of the bass vibrating through my bones. Big red letters hung over the entrance of a brick building.

Excitement flooded through me, and Keisha grabbed my hand, pulling me along beside her.

There was a huge line of people waiting to get into the club, but she walked us straight to the bouncer at the door.

She turned to me and winked. "Watch this."

She sidled up to the bouncer and ran a hand along his broad chest. "Hey there, big boy." She leaned into him as she ran her hand down to his tight stomach.

A black T-shirt that said Security on it hugged his big torso and was tucked into black pants. He had a smattering of tattoos on his arms and wore an earpiece that he occasionally spoke into.

With a deep baritone chuckle, he wrapped an arm around Keisha's shoulders. "Hello there, Keisha."

I shook my head and laughed.

Her eyes twinkled as she looked at me. "Kane, this is my friend, Tori. Tori, this is my favorite bouncer, Kane."

I smiled in greeting. Kane was huge and definitely was someone who I wouldn't want to be left alone with in an alley, that's for damn sure. His pale eyes were kind and gentle, but I bet he could kick some serious ass if needed.

"Well, any friend of my Keisha's, is a friend of mine." He smiled back at me. Blue eyes lit up every time he glanced at her, and I thought someone had a little crush on my new friend.

Our gazes met and she flushed.

I laughed.

Giggling, she freed herself from him.

He smiled down at her and looked between the two of us. "Have a good time, ladies." He stood back, motioning to the open doorway.

We headed through the door and walked down a dim, narrow hallway that had red lighting in the ceiling. Black-and-white pictures of famous musicians lined the walls on either side of us, and as we neared the end of the corridor, the music got louder. It wasn't so loud that I couldn't hear myself think or carry on a conversation, but loud enough that I felt the beat in the floor.

"Did you want to dance first or grab a drink?" Keisha yelled over the music.

"Drink first."

She nodded and led us to the bar.

Once we left the hallway, it opened up into a wide space. The bar was on the right and took up most of the wall that led to the back of the room.

To the left of us, there was a dance floor jam-packed with moving bodies. One cage in each corner held scantily clad women who gyrated and danced to the music.

Across the floor, on the other side of the club, red couches lined the wall. Some had curtains drawn closed for privacy.

The air in the room was thick and smelled of alcohol and sweat.

Keisha grabbed my hand, pulling me through the crowd, and led us to the bar. Once we reached it, we both took a seat.

The bartender noticed us, made a drink that looked like a martini, and placed it in front of her.

Wow. She knows everyone.

"Do you come here all of the time?" I asked her.

"Yeah, probably more than I should."

He nodded his head in my direction, and I looked at Keisha. "What do you want to drink?" she asked me.

"Oh, I'll have a beer, please." He nodded and a moment later placed a beer in front of me.

I grabbed the cool bottle and brought it to my lips. I took a long pull and sighed as the cold carbonated liquid slid down my throat.

"I've never seen someone make drinking beer look erotic."

My gaze flashed to Keisha's, and she smiled.

My cheeks felt hot, and I put my beer down. I shrugged. "I like beer."

She laughed. "Now I bet Sebastian would love seeing you drink beer that way."

I laughed, rolling my eyes.

I turned on my stool and scanned the vast room. The walls were black, and all of the lighting fixtures, except for the ones behind the bar, were some shade of red.

"Are you looking for Sebastian?" Keisha teased.

I smiled. "Maybe."

"Well, he does come here often, so you might see him, but be warned—he doesn't get along with my brother."

I frowned. "Why does that not surprise me?"

She laughed and turned on her stool. Leaning against the bar top, she crossed her legs. "Speaking of the owner…"

I followed her gaze and noticed a very good-looking man heading toward us. He was way better-looking in person than in the picture.

He wore a black dress shirt with sleeves rolled up to his elbows and black dress pants. I also noticed he was slim but looked fit, and his clothes hugged him in all the right places. He sauntered up to us, and the air around him crackled with authority.

Unlike Sebastian, this guy was clean-shaven with short no-fuss brown hair and no tattoos that I could see. They were completely different but I didn't feel for Brett what I felt for Sebastian.

He stopped in front of Keisha as she stood, and they hugged. Stepping back after their embrace, he held her at arm's length and looked down at her. "My, my, Keisha, you sure have gotten beautiful since the last time I saw you."

She rolled her eyes. "I saw you yesterday, Brett."

He laughed and pulled her in for another hug.

Keisha turned to me. "This is Brett McLean, my brother."

He held out his hand to me. "Stepbrother." His eyes were warm and inviting, kind of like a sauna.

I shook his hand. That explained the two different last names and how they looked nothing alike.

Keisha rolled her eyes. "Whatever. And Brett, this Tori McLeod. We met a couple of weeks ago at my job, and I decided to bring her out tonight. She's a regular customer," Keisha added before taking a sip of her martini.

I nodded in agreement. "I have a thing for coffee."

"And beer."

I laughed. "Yes and beer."

"We definitely have lots of beer. Well, I'm glad you ladies decided to come here. So Tori…" Brett said, smiling at me. His eyes, even though the room was a shade of red, were the brightest shade of blue I had ever seen.

"She's taken," Keisha announced, glaring at him.

My gaze snapped to Keisha's. I wasn't taken. If Brett had asked me out, I probably would have said yes.

"What?" she asked innocently.

I huffed and turned back to Brett.

He smiled but didn't finish his sentence.

Sighing, I motioned for the bartender, and he placed another beer in front of me without me having to ask. I think I like this guy.

I smiled to myself as I took a swig and sighed.

"You did it again!"

My eyes snapped open. I hadn't even realized that I had closed them. I coughed and lightly smacked Keisha on the arm, sending her into a fit of giggles.

"What did you do?" Brett asked.

"Nothing!" I cried, and that caused Keisha to laugh even harder. I felt Brett's stare bore into my side, causing my face to heat up.

"So Brett, how long have you owned the club?"

We made small talk while Keisha controlled her giggles. I learned that Brett had bought the club as soon as he turned twenty-one. He had wanted to be a business owner all his life, and having a club seemed like the best thing for him at the time. He admitted to me that he had originally invested in the club to win over ladies, but eventually the club became a part of him.

"So are you in school?" he asked me.

"Well…kind of."

He chuckled. "You don't seem too sure about that."

I laughed. "I had to take some time off to look for a job, but I hope to go back next year even though it's boring. Now I just need to find something so I can pay back my school loans."

He smiled at me. "Well I hope you find one. Let me know if you have difficulty, though. We always need extra people here."

My eyes widened. "Wow, really? Thank you. I hope I can find a position on my own, but I'll definitely keep that in mind."

He nodded and leaned forward. "Keisha, Garrith has been asking about you."

Keisha turned to him, her cheeks coloring, and she continued sipping her drink.

Brett laughed and leaned back in his chair.

"Who's Garrith?" I asked her.

She sighed. "He's a friend of Brett's, and it's a long story."

"Oh." Now that was a story I wanted to hear. She chewed her bottom lip and continued sipping her drink. I felt for her. There must have been some sort of history between the two of them, and I hoped that when she was ready she would tell me.

"He's a good friend of mine, and he has a thing for Keisha, but she's not interested," Brett interjected.

She scoffed. "He's obnoxious and an ass, but I never said that I wasn't interested."

"I think you need to give me details later," I said to her.

She turned to me and winked. "Definitely."

"You have got to be fucking kidding me." Brett growled.

My head whipped around as he looked toward the door, scowling.

Keisha and I both followed his gaze.

"What?" we asked in unison.

My eyes scanned the vast room around us, but I didn't see anything out of the ordinary. People danced, people drank, chatted… It all seemed like a normal club to me.

Brett's jaw tightened. "Remember that fucker I told you about, Keisha?"

"Sebastian? Yes, I remember," Keisha answered.

My face heated at the mention of his name.

"How do you know his name?" Brett frowned.

"Um…" Keisha looked away.

"I told her his name," I said, not understanding what the issue was.

His gaze snapped to mine. "How do you know his name?"

"That's not important. Continue what you were going to say," Keisha interrupted.

"No. Tori, how do you know him?"

Anxious butterflies started fluttering about in my stomach. What was this guy's issue? "Well I don't think that's any of your…"

"Brett. Stop being an overprotective asshole."

He scowled at his sister. "I'm not being an overprotective asshole."

"Yes, you are. You just met Tori. You can't tell her who she can and can't hang out with."

My nerves rattled at the hard look on Brett's face. What was his problem with Sebastian? Maybe I should have been concerned, but something about him had me drawn to him. For whatever reason it was, I trusted him. Even not knowing a single thing about Sebastian, my body didn't seem to care as it responded to even just the mere mention of his name.

Brett sighed and turned away. Reaching a hand up to his ear, he started whispering.

Keisha continued, not noticing. "If he's that much of an issue, kick him out. It's your club."

A moment later, Brett turned back to us. "I can't kick him out. He hasn't done anything wrong. I just don't trust the guy."

Keisha rolled her eyes. "So what does he have to do with anything, then?"

"He's here, that's what." He nodded towards the door. "And it pisses me off that I can't do anything about it."

My heart fluttered in my chest, knowing that I would get to see him again. I searched through the crowd again but couldn't see him. My body hummed in anticipation, and my skin heated as I remembered that he now knew where I lived.

"Holy shit." Keisha exclaimed, stifling a giggle.

We both turned to her, and as she looked at me, a small smile formed on her lips. "Um…Tori. Brett's right. Sebastian is here."

My eyes went wide. "What? Where?"

"By the door. He just came in." She pointed to the entrance.

I quickly scanned the area by the entrance, but I didn't see him. Then the crowd parted for a brief moment, and I saw him leaning against the wall talking to someone. He looked gorgeous as always, still wearing his black leather jacket, T-shirt and jeans.

My stomach jumped, and my heart sped up against my chest.

"I tried telling you he was here. Tori, you really should stay away from him." Brett warned.

Keisha rolled her eyes. "You men and your territory issues. Tori, ignore him. I'm sure he's not that bad, now, is he Brett?"

He scoffed. "Yeah, okay. Listen, Tori, just be careful. Please."

I turned back to Brett, and his jaw clenched. "Brett, I promise that I'll be careful, but I don't think you have anything to worry about."

"Tori?"

I looked at Keisha.

"I think he knows you're here."

My eyes snapped up. He was looking right at me.

CHAPTER FIVE

I LOOKED AWAY AND turned back to Brett, but I could still feel Sebastian's gaze boring into the back of my skull.

"I can't fucking stand that guy." Brett scowled.

Keisha huffed. "We get that. Can we move on now?"

I looked between the two of them and then hopped off the stool, needing some air. Since finding out Sebastian was there, it felt like all of the oxygen had been sucked out of the club. Even being across the room from him, I felt a pull towards him.

"Where are you going?" they both asked me.

Turning back to them, I rolled my eyes. "If you must know, I'm going to the washroom. Did you want a play-by-play when I get back?"

Brett turned to Keisha. "I think I like her. She's feisty."

She glared at him. Her eyes widened when they flicked back to mine. A grin spread on her face as she looked past me.

Brett muttered something that I didn't hear as he rose from his seat.

Frowning, I turned on my heel and ran right into a hard body. My hands instinctively landed on the chest, bracing my fall. I gasped and looked up into black eyes.

Sebastian.

The familiar smell of cologne and soap invaded my nostrils, and it was just as intoxicating as before. My core clenched, aching for him.

Grabbing my wrists, he rubbed his thumb over my pulse point.

My breath picked up, and my heart thundered against my chest as I watched the small movement. My gaze flashed up to his, and a small smile formed on his lips.

"Hello, Tori." His deep, silky voice washed over me, caressing my skin as he continued to rub small circles on my wrist.

"Hi," I said, hardly able to breathe. It had been weeks since I had seen him, and being this close to him made my insides turn to mush.

He let go of my wrists and tucked a strand of hair behind my ear.

Shivers ran down my spine at the light, feathery touch. My nipples hardened against my bra, turning to sharp peaks, begging to be touched by him.

"Come here often?" His deep voice sent a current of electrifying pleasure through me. This guy was going to do damage to my self-control.

"Does that sort of pickup line work on every girl, or is this your first time testing it out?" I laughed, asking the same question I had asked him the first time we met.

He chuckled. "That depends."

"On?" I asked, playing along.

"Is it working?" His voice lowered and he leaned down, hot breath grazing my ear.

My heart thumped a mile a minute against my chest; I thought it would explode. A sharp pain pinched my ear, and then I realized he'd bitten me. Liquid heat seeped between my legs at the unexpected contact.

Oh God. My eyes went wide. Did I say that aloud?

He lifted his head and looked down at me, eyes blazing. Placing his hand on the small of my back, he pulled me against his side. He winked at me. "So is it?"

I frowned, confused. "Is what?"

"Is it working?"

My stomach flip-flopped. "Oh…" Yes, it was very much indeed working, but there was no way that I was telling him that.

A cough sounded from behind us, and I turned around. Keisha had the biggest smile, one that lit up her whole face.

Brett's face was hard as he glared daggers at Sebastian. He took a couple of steps toward us. "Sebastian Chelios." His voice was thick with disgust.

Sebastian placed his hand on my hip, pulling me closer to him. Interesting.

"So, Brett, the club is booming as always," Sebastian drawled.

I could sense a hint of sarcasm in his voice.

"I…" Brett looked to his left and shook his head slightly but not before Sebastian and I caught the movement.

"Got your boys watching me, do you?" Sebastian's body tensed as if he was bracing himself for a fight. Brett was smaller than him, but with Kane, Sebastian didn't have a chance.

I looked between the two men and felt the tension rolling off them. "Guys. Stop."

Brett folded his arms and glared. "Are you going to give me a reason to, asshole?"

Sebastian tensed beside me.

I turned my body to him and hooked my hands around his arm. "Sebastian?"

His jaw clenched and unclenched, and he took a step toward Brett.

"Hey." I grabbed his jacket, stopping him.

"Brett, why don't you buy me a drink?" I jumped at the sound of Keisha's voice, not having seen her move from her chair.

"We don't pay for drinks," Brett bit out, standing toe-to-toe with Sebastian.

"Just come have a drink with me, ass. Seriously." Keisha pulled on his arm.

Brett continued to stare down Sebastian. His glare flashed toward me and something showed in it. Jealousy? Warning? I didn't know. But whatever it was made my stomach tighten.

Ignoring him, I intertwined my hand in Sebastian's, making him look down at me, finally. "Dance with me."

He seemed to think this over, and a moment later his gaze darkened. He looked back at Brett, and a wicked glint flashed in his eyes. Releasing my hand, he pulled off his leather jacket, which revealed a tight black T-shirt that seemed molded to his hard torso.

I tried not to stare at the tattoos which covered arms that were huge, like he worked out daily. I also couldn't help but notice how the beautiful artwork went all the way down to his fingers.

He placed his jacket on a nearby table and turned to me.

I looked away as my face heated at being caught staring at him.

He walked up to me and grabbed my chin. The pad of his thumb ran over my bottom lip. "Don't be embarrassed about staring at me." He leaned down to my ear. "I fucking love it when your eyes are on my body."

He placed a kiss on my neck, grabbed my hand, and brushed his lips across my knuckles.

My heart stuttered and I didn't respond.

He laughed and walked me to the dance floor, his arm going around my shoulders.

My phone vibrated, and I fished it out of my clutch. I turned on the screen and quickly read, Be careful. Need anything, Kane will be there. Brett. I rolled my eyes but also appreciated his overprotectiveness.

Putting my phone away, I saw Kane standing against the wall by a set of double doors. He winked at me and I smiled back. I gave him a little wave as we walked by.

As we approached the dance floor, butterflies flew around in my belly. What had possessed me to ask Sebastian to dance with me? I only ever danced in my living room, where no one was around to judge, and that's it. But dancing with a gorgeous man who obviously knew how to use his body was probably not a smart idea on my part.

We walked through the sweating, gyrating bodies and found a clear spot on the dance floor.

Sebastian moved behind me, and pulled me against his body. He placed his hands on my hips and moved me to the loud music that came out of the speakers.

The bass line of the music pumped through my blood as we danced to the fast beat.

I became so entranced at the feel of him touching me again that I could only focus on the feel of his hands on my hips, so I no longer danced.

Hot, wet kisses started at my shoulder and moved to my neck, sending shivers straight to my core. Pleasure coursed through me as a warm tongue licked the soft spot just under my ear. I leaned my head to the side to give him easier access to my skin.

I placed my hands on top of his and began moving my hips to the beat again. Luckily we were surrounded by people who were dancing the same as we were. I wasn't sure if it was the beer or just Sebastian himself, but I lost all willpower when it came to him. My body desired him, and for some odd reason, it didn't scare me or concern me. No man had ever made me feel the way Sebastian did.

A sense of bravery washed over me, and I started grinding against his pelvis. I smiled as his hands tightened on my hips.

My heart beat fast against my chest, and I turned my head just as he lifted his. My lips parted in anticipation.

He turned me around and I placed my hands on his chest as we continued to move to the beat of the music. His hands moved from my hips to my ass and pulled me tighter against him.

I smoothed my hands down the soft cotton of his shirt to his waist. His breath hitched as I ran a hand under the soft fabric, fingers grazing over his tight stomach. Hooking my fingers in the waistband of his jeans, I ran them along the soft skin just under his belly button.

He looked at me through hooded eyes and moved one hand to the small of my back, my skin igniting at the touch. I could feel him through my thin tank top and I wanted more. I craved it.

Running my hand to his back, I stuck it in his back jean pocket and pulled him against me.

Sebastian smirked and kept his hand on my back, moving the other one to pinch my chin. He held it firmly in place while the pad of his thumb grazed over my bottom lip.

My mouth parted as my breathing quickened.

He leaned down, licked my bottom lip, and gently bit it, sending bolts of electricity to my groin. Liquid pooled in my panties, and I grabbed his waistband with both hands, pulling him against me.

He grinned and covered my mouth with his, shoving his tongue between my lips. I moaned as he devoured me, taking full control. Owning me.

It felt so good to be kissing him again. It felt familiar. His warm, soft lips pressed roughly against mine, spread tingles over my skin.

He ran his hand up my spine to the back of my neck, sending shivers along with it. Sebastian released my mouth and trailed soft kisses on the corner of my lips, along my jaw and to my ear.

His hot breath on my skin made my eyes flutter closed as I leaned into him. "Sebastian." I breathed his name, not knowing if he could hear me over the loud music. I opened my eyes as he lifted his head.

He looked down at me, his eyes full of hunger as he ran his thumb over my bottom lip. Leaning down to my ear, his hot breath scorched my skin. "I want to fuck you."

My stomach flip-flopped. Did I hear him right? Oh God.

Opening my mouth, my teeth lightly grazed his thumb as it ran over my lips. I smiled as his nostrils flared.

A moment later he looked up and frowned. The hunger in his gaze turned to anger and then rage. He looked back down at me and placed a firm kiss on my lips. Grabbing my hand from his waist, he tugged me from the dancing crowd.

Confusion coursed through me as I followed him.

He pushed through the crowd of dancing bodies as he pulled me along.

"Sebastian."

He turned back to me.

"What's wrong?" Concern for him ran through me as I walked quickly to keep up with him.

His mouth was set in a grim line, and his body was tense. Something was seriously off with him. No longer being the playful Sebastian I had come to know, he took on a harder edge that made nervous butterflies soar through my belly.

"Where are you taking me?"

He didn't respond as we walked past Brett and Keisha.

They looked at me, concern etched in their features, but I just shrugged and ran to keep up with Sebastian.

Sebastian grabbed his jacket before we headed to the exit. We stopped once we neared a man leaning against the wall. Sebastian still had my hand in a tight grip and kept me close against him.

Worry and anxiety burned through me, but I didn't say anything else or ask Sebastian any more questions.

I ran my other hand up and down his arm, and he looked down at me, eyes softening.

"Well, well, well. Now what do we have here?"

Sebastian's head snapped up.

The man who had been leaning against the wall came toward us. His black eyes were partially hidden behind shaggy black hair, making him look even scarier. He was tall and lean and pretty much dressed the same as Sebastian.

I moved closer to Sebastian as the guy stopped in front of us.

The other guy's black eyes bored into mine and roamed over my body. "So is this what you've been doing all this time?"

Sebastian's hand tightened against mine, and I squeezed it in reassurance.

This guy radiated pure evil. He looked down at me, no emotion showing on his face.

My heart started pounding.

He looked around as if he was searching for something. He seemed on edge and twitchy, and it made me very uncomfortable. His gaze darted back to mine and as it travelled up and down my body, it made my skin crawl.

He was smaller than Sebastian but gave off the same dominating air. Tattoos peeked out from under the collar of his T-shirt as well, much like Sebastian's.

"Like what you see, cochina?" His deep, slightly accented voice set my nerves on edge.

"What are you doing here, Jose?" Sebastian asked, his voice laced with venom.

"I could ask you the same thing, but I guess it's pretty obvious now isn't it?" Jose bit out.

Sebastian took a step closer to him, but I firmly held his hand, pulling him back.

Jose's eyebrow rose. "Ah, I see you have your slut calling the shots now. You must be pussy-whipped."

I glared at Jose, instantly hating him. "Who the hell do you think you are?"

He sneered. "Sebastian, you've changed, my man. You never would have let a whore come between us."

"Fuck you, Jose. She's not a whore." Sebastian released my hand and pushed me behind him, taking another step towards Jose.

"Yup, definitely pussy-whipped."

Sebastian swung at Jose and hit him in the jaw, snapping his head to the side.

Jose turned back to him and laughed. "That's all you got? Man, you've been out of the game for too long."

He continued laughing as Sebastian geared up to hit him again.

I grabbed his arm. "Sebastian, he isn't worth it."

"Yeah, Sebastian, listen to your slut."

Anger burned in my belly at being called a slut one too many times. Before I knew what I was doing, I dove at Jose.

Arms encircled my waist before I could hit him, but the shock on his face was satisfying enough…for the moment.

The look of surprise instantly switched to fury behind Jose's black eyes. "Get control of your girl, before I do it for you, asshole."

Sebastian growled behind me and I tried pushing his hands off me. My body shook with anger. I wanted a piece of Jose. I want to punch that slimy grin off his face. No one called me a slut and got away with it. I didn't care who they were.

Jose tossed a cell phone at Sebastian. "I'll be calling you, and you'd better fucking answer it. You don't want me to come after you if you don't." Jose turned and stormed down the hall leading to the exit.

I turned to Sebastian, releasing myself from his grip. "What the hell was that about, and who the hell is that guy? And what's with the phone?"

Sebastian placed his hand on the back of my neck. "Breath, baby. He's a douche-bag. No one important." He frowned, shoving the phone in his pocket. "He'll call me when he needs something."

Confusion coursed through me as I wondered what the history was between Jose and him. "Why didn't you let me hit him?" I asked, trying to lighten the mood.

"Because he wouldn't think twice before hitting you back," he said through clenched teeth, seething with anger.

My stomach rolled at that thought. "Oh."

"Everything all right here?"

I turned and saw Kane, Brett, and Keisha standing around us.

Sebastian ran a hand through his hair. "Yeah, everything is fine. I dealt with it."

He grabbed the back of my neck and kissed my forehead. My body relaxed at that simple touch. I was safe. Jose was no longer there, so I didn't have to worry about him any longer.

"Did you actually dive at that guy, Tori?" Keisha asked me, interrupting my thoughts.

I looked at Sebastian and then back at her. "Yeah, I did."

Her eyes widened, and she pulled me in for a hug. "Wow, you go, girl. You're kind of crazy, but I love it."

"Keisha," Brett admonished.

"What? I gotta give props to my girl." She rolled her eyes and hugged me again.

I smiled slightly. It would've been better if I had gotten a couple of shots in at least.

"I think you should leave." Brett crossed his arms under his chest and scowled at Sebastian.

"Brett." Keisha smacked him on the arm. "That guy isn't here anymore. It's no longer a problem."

Ignoring his sister, he continued to glare at Sebastian. "Leave. Now."

"Listen, Jose showing up here tonight was not my fault. He's not supposed to be back in town," Sebastian told him.

"Doesn't matter. He's not allowed here and you know that, so I think you should leave before we forcibly remove you."

"We meaning Kane? Maybe you should do it yourself, Brett? Be a man for once in your life, and show me how you really feel about me." Sebastian took a step toward him.

Oh…this is not going to be good.

"All right guys, that's enough." Kane clapped a hand on Brett's shoulder and handed Sebastian his jacket. "Sebastian, leave."

"You can't make me leave," Sebastian argued, taking the coat from him.

Brett took a step toward him so that they were almost standing toe-to-toe. "Wanna bet?"

I moved between them, pushing them apart. "Seriously, guys. Stop."

Sebastian looked down at me. "I should go. Don't want any issues for pretty boy over here."

Disappointment fluttered through me. "I can come with you."

"No, stay here, just in case Jose is still lurking around." Sebastian cupped the back of my neck and pulled me toward him. My blood boiled at that, and Sebastian smiled. "You sure are feisty when you're mad, little one. It's kinda hot."

I rolled my eyes and laughed, wrapping my arms around his waist.

He looked up, his eyes narrowing. "Do you mind?"

I followed his gaze and saw Brett huff. He grabbed Keisha's arm, and they walked back to the bar with Kane beside them, but not before he gave Sebastian a death glare.

Sebastian chuckled and pulled me against him, enveloping me in an embrace.

"You like getting under Brett's skin don't you?"

"Yes, I do. Very much so, actually."

I laughed, and then questions started flashing through my mind. "What happened with you and him?"

Sebastian ran his fingers through his hair, making my breath catch at the sight. "Bad business gone wrong. Long story. I don't want to bore you with the details."

He grabbed my chin and tilted it up toward him. Placing a firm kiss on my lips, his dark eyes flashed with concern.

I frowned. "Sebastian."

He cleared his throat and brushed his lips softly against mine. "I'll call you, little one."

Releasing me, he walked out of the club. Cold chills ran up my spine, and I rubbed my arms. So many questions ran through my mind, but I couldn't get Jose out of my head. The way he'd looked at me set my nerves on edge.

As much as he infuriated me, he scared the hell out of me even more, and I had a feeling that tonight wouldn't be the last I heard from him.

CHAPTER SIX

I WALKED BACK TO the bar and saw Keisha sitting by herself. "Where's Brett?"

She turned to me. "He's in his office sulking."

I sat down beside her and sighed. "Well…didn't I say that tonight would be interesting?"

"Yeah, you did. Next time, how about you not say that."

I laughed. "Good idea."

We sat in silence for a moment. After my encounters with Sebastian, my attraction toward him didn't just simmer. Every time I saw him, my desire for him grew and grew. He controlled my thoughts and my dreams.

"Are you ok?"

I looked at Keisha. Concern marked her features. "Yeah, I'm fine. But I think another drink is in order."

"Sounds good to me, girlfriend."

Instead of the drinks we had earlier, Keisha ordered us some shots. The bartender placed them in front of us.

I picked up the small glass and turned to Keisha. "Here's to a new beginning."

She raised her glass, clinking it against mine. "And to no more drama."

We both downed the clear liquid. It burned my throat as I swallowed, but it wasn't too intense. A warm feeling coated my skin as the alcohol settled in my belly.

"Want another one?" she asked.

"Sure."

The bartender placed two more in front of us, and we clinked glasses again and downed the dark liquid. I wiped the corner of my lips and sucked the drops off of my finger.

"I think I'm in love with Mr. Tequila." Keisha giggled.

I laughed. "I think I am too. Barkeep, another round of shots for me and my lovely lady friend here, please."

He smiled and poured us more shots.

"No." Keisha slammed her shot glass on the bar top. "You my dear friend, are in love with that fine-ass man Sebastian."

I coughed, the tequila in my belly threatening to rise to my throat. Clearly, she'd had too much to drink. "I think you are cut off, Keisha."

Her eyes widened, and she swayed a little on her stool. "Yeah, maybe I am."

We'd had the same number of shots, but they were obviously affecting Keisha a lot more than me, so I helped her off her stool, but all the alcohol seemed to rush to my head.

Grabbing onto the bar top, I tried catching my balance.

Keisha giggled. "I think you had too much to drink too."

I nodded, breathing through my mouth as my stomach churned.

Keisha grabbed my hand, and we walked to Brett's office leaning on each other for support. By the time we reached it, we were both in hysterics.

The door opened, and Brett stood in the doorway frowning, looking between us. "Are you guys drunk?"

"No," we said at the same time, making us laugh even harder.

Brett sighed. "Come on."

He pulled both of us into his office and shut the door.

We walked to one of the couches in the middle of the small room and plopped down with me practically sitting on Keisha's lap. She pushed me off her, and I giggled.

Keisha curled in the corner of the couch and lay down, resting her head on the arm of the seat.

"I think she's gonna pass out."

"Yeah, probably." Brett placed a blanket on her and went to the minibar. Bringing us both back a bottle of water, he sat on the couch across from me.

I took a swig of mine, placed it on the table in front of me, and removed my heels. Rubbing my feet, I sighed, not realizing how much the shoes hurt until they came off the feet.

"Here, let me."

I stopped mid-rub and saw Brett standing before me. I watched him as he sat on the table directly in front of me. "Lean back."

I did as he said and leaned back against the couch, placing my feet in his lap.

He grabbed one of my feet, straightening my leg, and I jumped as his thumbs pushed into the arch of my foot.

I tried not to giggle as he unintentionally tickled me.

"Stop squirming." His laughter lit up his eyes, and I joined him with my giggles.

"But it tickles."

He pressed harder and the ticklishness went away. "Does that still tickle?"

"No," I said.

Oh God, that feels good.

His fingers pressed and moved over my foot, removing the aching tingles from my heels.

My eyes closed and I reveled in the feel of his thumb pressing into the arch of my foot. Delicious shivers shot up my leg to my groin.

Sebastian.

My eyes shot open. Sebastian should be giving me a foot massage, not Brett. What was I thinking? I removed my foot from his grasp. "Thank you."

"You didn't let me do the other one," Brett said, reaching for my other foot.

I sat up. I didn't feel comfortable having him touch me. It was only a foot massage, but it felt more intimate than what I had wanted. "It's fine."

"It's because of Sebastian, isn't it?"

I nodded.

"You guys aren't even together," he grumbled.

I glared at him. "Thank you for that reminder, Brett. Either way, it still doesn't feel right." His jaw clenched and unclenched, and even though I was drunk, I knew something was up. "What?"

He scrubbed a hand down his face as if he was bracing himself for my reaction—or he was just doing it to buy time. Maybe he didn't really care how I would react. "If you're going to be friends with my sister, you need to stay the fuck away from Sebastian."

My eyes widened. "Excuse me? I think Keisha should be the one to decide who she hangs out with or not."

"I don't want her hurt. If something happened to her…I…" He paused.

I smiled sympathetically. "Brett, nothing is going to happen to her."

"You don't know that!"

"Okay, seriously?" Shock tore through me at how he was acting. I would never deliberately hurt Keisha. She was like the sister I never had. We'd become fast friends, and I would do anything for her.

Keisha stirred and Brett lowered his voice. "I know Sebastian and Jose. You need to stay away from them. If you don't, I can't allow you to see Keisha anymore."

Anger burned in my belly, and I rose to my feet. "Keisha's right. You are an overprotective asshole."

"Tori, I'm just trying to look out for her. She's the only family I have left." He scrubbed his face and leaned his elbows on his knees.

"Trust me, if anything happened to her, I'd go after him myself."

Brett frowned, like he was hesitating to say what he really wanted. "It's not just Jose I'm referring to."

"Leave Sebastian out of this." I grabbed my clutch and headed to the door. "I should go home."

"Tori." He rose from his seat and walked toward me. "Just be careful. Please."

I turned to him and crossed my arms over my chest.

He pulled me into an embrace. "I know Keisha likes you, and I'm happy that she finally found a new friend but…"

"Nothing will happen to her," I reiterated.

He sighed. "I wish you weren't so fucking naïve."

I pushed against him, releasing myself from his arms, and frowned. "I am not naïve."

"Whatever, Tori. I'm not going to argue with you."

I rolled my eyes and opened the door.

"I'm not letting you leave alone when you're drunk," he said, grabbing my arm.

Glaring at him, I wobbled on my feet. "Fine. Are you going to walk me home, then?"

"Yes." He pulled out a cell phone and called Kane, asking him to stay with Keisha while he stepped out.

Kane showed up a couple of moments later, a bounce in his step that he got to take care of her.

I giggled and then left Brett's office, not bothering to wait for him. Who the hell did he think he was anyway? He had no right telling me not to hang out with his sister.

"We can head out this way," Brett said, coming up beside me. We turned down a long hall that had an Exit sign above it and stepped out in the early-morning air.

My phone started ringing, and I quickly pulled it out of my clutch.

Brett placed his hand on my lower back, guiding me to the sidewalk.

"Hello?" No one responded as static came from the other end.

"Hello?" I said again and looked up at Brett.

"Who is it?" he asked.

"I'm not sure… Hello?" Still no answer. I sighed and was about to hang up when deep breathing came over the line.

"You better not fucking hang up on me."

I frowned. "Who the hell is this?"

"Who do you think, cochina?"

My blood ran cold. "Jose."

"Who the hell is it?" Brett asked.

"Wow, you sure are quick." Jose chuckled.

"How did you get my number?" Goose pimples coated my skin and I quickened my pace.

"That's not important. What is important, though, is I need you to get Sebastian to meet with me."

"And you think I have control over him?"

"Oh, no, cochina. You definitely don't, but when I call him, he'll refuse to see me, so I need you to convince him otherwise."

I breathed a sigh of relief as I saw my apartment building in the near distance. "And what if I don't do that?"

There was a pause on the other end. "Then I'll just have to come to you. That'll convince him enough."

I stopped in my tracks, my heart beating hard against my chest. "Please, as if…"

"I don't suggest stopping in this area. It's not very safe. Tell Brett he better take care of you. You never know what's lurking in the dark."

My eyes widened as the phone went dead.

CHAPTER SEVEN

AFTER JOSE HUNG UP on me, I quickly walked the rest of the way home. I told Brett who had called and what Jose had said. Brett made sure I got home safely and then headed quickly back to the club to check on Keisha.

Not knowing where Jose was but knowing that he could see us while we were walking down the street made my anxiety level soar to new levels I never experienced before. My lungs were burning, and I was panting from overexertion as I reached my apartment.

I checked my cell phone before placing it on the hall table. I had no new messages.

Thank God.

My place was small, only having one very tiny bedroom, but it was home, and it was all I could afford as a student anyway.

I walked to my couch and plopped down. Looking at the clock on my DVD player, I saw that it was only three thirty a.m.

I heard a collar jingle as my cat, Rooster, approached me. Jumping up on the coffee table, his big, long body took up quite a bit of space when he lay down. Being the runt of the litter I got him from, he was smaller than most Maine coons, but he was still larger than an average house cat.

"Good morning, Rooster." I scratched his head and ran my fingers through his orange and white fur, starting his purr motor.

I rose from the couch and headed to the kitchen to feed him. Afterwards, I turned and headed to my bedroom, stripping on the way. Grabbing a tank top out of my dresser drawer, I threw it on when a cold draft stopped me. I turned to my window and frowned. Shivers ran over my body, and I shook myself.

There's nothing to be scared of, Tori.

I quickly ran to my window and slammed it shut, locking it in place. Turning to my bed, images of Sebastian flashed through my mind, and I sighed.

It was going to be a long-ass night.

***

Hot, wet kisses trailed from my ear to my neck and back up to my jaw. I moaned as a mouth covered mine, tongue diving between my lips. Our tongues duelled and danced, igniting my skin on fire.

I recognized the mouth on mine. It felt familiar, but I couldn't quite place where I'd felt these lips before. Was I dreaming? I must have been. There was no way he would show up like this unannounced…or maybe he would.

My dream lover released my mouth and a hand grabbed my jaw, holding it tightly in place. He then slammed his lips back down on mine as he kissed me more forcefully. My lips tingled at the rough impact, but I sighed deeply at the pleasure coursing through my body.

The mouth sucked and pulled at my bottom lip before covering mine again.

I reached up and ran my hands through the hair at the nape of my lover, and pulled him harder against me, releasing a deep growl from him.

The hand moved from my jaw to my bare breast. A thumb ran over my nipple, and the peak instantly hardened under his touch. He squeezed the bud between his fingers, igniting a sharp pain that shot straight to my clit, and I cried out against his mouth.

Releasing me, he asked, "Do you like that, little one?"
Sebastian.

I was dreaming about Sebastian. Well, this was new. My brain was foggy as I tried to make him out, but my eyes couldn't focus, so I reveled in the touch of his hands on my body.

I moaned in response, and he squeezed my nipple again, almost making me come undone against his hand.

He chuckled lightly. Moving his hand from my nipple, his fingers roamed down my ribs, over my stomach, and stopped just before reaching the place I wanted him most.

"Please." I breathed. "Touch me."

His hand reached over my mound, finger caressing between my wet folds, lightly stroking my clit. I arched and cried out. His mouth came back down on mine as two fingers entered my...

I bolted upright in bed as my alarm went off. Grabbing my phone, I quickly turned it off and lay back down, chest pumping.

Wow. Now he has me dreaming of him?

Grumbling to myself, I blamed Sebastian for the very naughty and hot dream. Oh, wouldn't he love it if he found out that I was dreaming of him too?

Taking a couple of deep breaths, I tried to form coherent thoughts, even though my brain was still fuzzy from my very unsatisfying dream.

I was a little bothered that I had dreamt of Sebastian, but right now I ached so badly with need that I couldn't concentrate.

My loins tingled and my nipples hardened just thinking about my dream. Why couldn't I have slept just a little bit longer? If I'd had his number, at that point my body would have overruled any conscious thought I had and I'd call him. I needed him so badly that I shook from lack of release.

I closed my eyes as the images from my dream flowed through my mind. I ran my hands under my shirt and up to my full breasts. I squeezed my nipple between my fingers like Sebastian did in my dream, causing me to cry out.

My other hand ran over my stomach and grazed the top of my panties. I kept my eyes closed as I imagined Sebastian touching me.

Releasing my breast, I took off my panties and placed my hands on my bent knees. I took a couple of deep breaths as I lay there for a moment.

Why hadn't he given me his number? Sighing in frustration, I closed my eyes again and slowly ran one hand down my thigh. I gasped as I lightly caressed my slick center, running my finger up over my clit and back down again. I inserted a finger and moaned.

Running it back up to my clit, I flicked it gently but firmly, imagining it was Sebastian making me feel this way.

Tingles started from my toes and travelled up my body as I felt the ecstasy building.

I flicked my clit harder and faster as an orgasm exploded from my middle, making me scream Sebastian's name.

***

After my very unsatisfying self-induced orgasm, I hoped that Sebastian would call me and call me soon.

I rummaged through my clothes, deciding that I needed to go shopping eventually. While I was searching for an outfit to wear to go job hunting, my cell rang. I threw my clothes down, accidentally hitting Rooster, and ran to my phone. "Sorry, baby."

I picked it up and didn't recognize the number on the call display. I swiped my finger across the touch screen and placed it up to my ear. "Hello?"

"Hello, Tori?"

"Yes, this is she."

"Oh, good. I'm so sorry for calling you this early."

I looked at my clock. It read 8:28 a.m. I shrugged. "Oh, it's not too early at all. How can I help you?"

"This is Melanie Atkinson…"

"Oh. Hi!" I recognized the name from an application I'd filled out weeks ago. It was for an office assistant position with some big corporation. It wasn't much, but it would help pay the bills while I figured out what I wanted to do with my life, and it would help me be able to afford to go back to school.

"I was calling to offer you the position."

"Yes, please! I'll take it!" Overjoyed, I danced around my bedroom while still holding the phone to my ear.

Melanie laughed. "Wonderful. So the hours are Monday through Friday, nine a.m. to five p.m."

She proceeded to tell me that I would be starting a week from tomorrow. I would also have benefits, free taxi vouchers, too, if I had to stay late. Those weren't needed since I lived close. Since I didn't have a car, the job was in the perfect location.

I hung up with Melanie and placed my phone back on my nightstand.

Walking to the bathroom, I started taking off my shirt when my cell phone rang again. I picked up my phone, noticing an unknown number again. "Hello?"

I waited for a response but heard nothing on the other end. "Hellooo?"

Still getting no response from the other end, I hung up. "Whatever."

I threw my phone on my bed and walked to the bathroom. I lifted my top over my head and threw it on the floor.

Turning on the light, I was about to start the shower when someone started banging on my apartment door. I jumped, quickly threw on my housecoat, and ran to my door. Goose pimples coated my skin as my heart thudded against my chest.

I looked out my tiny peephole and saw no one. Taking a deep breath, I unlocked my door and opened it slowly, and of course, no one was there. Why would someone be there? That would only make sense since someone knocked on the door. I rolled my eyes at myself and closed the door, locked it and double-checked it this time.

I think I've been watching too many scary movies.

CHAPTER EIGHT

MY PHONE RANG AS I shut off the shower. Grabbing my towel, I threw it around me and ran to my cell. I gasped as water dripped down my spine from my wet hair, sending cold shivers up my body. "Hello?"

"Mmm…now that's a nice sound to hear when you call someone."

My skin heated at the deep, smooth voice from the other end of the phone. He was calling me. Oh God. If only he would have called me an hour ago. He could be in my bed or on my floor, or even against the wall would work, too. Any way with him probably worked. Shaking my head, I realized I didn't respond to his greeting. "Hello, Sebastian."

"Hello, little one. So, did I catch you at a bad time?"

It was perfect timing, actually, since I was standing there naked, talking to the man from my dreams. My cheeks heated at that memory. "No, I was just in the shower."

"Now that is a wonderful image."

I laughed, which more in turn sounded like a nervous giggle. God, this guy had me falling all over myself for him. I just needed him, once. That would get him out of my system. Wouldn't it? Probably not.

"Were you thinking of me?" he asked huskily. He was cocky, and even if I denied it, he would know I was lying. He knew I was attracted to him, or else I wouldn't have given him my address and phone number.

Sitting on the edge of the bed, I cleared my throat. "Wouldn't you like to know?"

He chuckled. "Yes, I would actually. So were you?"

I was going to deny it, but thought maybe he would enjoy it more if I was honest. "Yes, I was thinking of you, Sebastian."

Sebastian coughed. "Wow…I wasn't expecting you to say that."

Feeling quite proud of myself, I mentally cheered. "Did I throw you off your game?"

"Yeah, I think you did." I could picture him running a hand through his messy hair, his big bicep bulging under the strain of his shirt. I licked my lips at the mental image.

Satisfied that I had knocked him down a peg or two, I simply said, "Good."

"Oh, little one. We sure are feisty, aren't we?" Amusement coated his voice. "So was your shower lonely?"

Holy shit. I shook myself and cleared my throat. "Nope. Not at all. Why would it be?"

"Because I wasn't with you."

My heart sped up. I knew that was the reason, but I just wanted to hear him say it. "Oh. I didn't even notice."

He laughed. "You're so full of shit."

I smiled. He knew me well already. "Am I now?"

"Yes you are, and I bet you dream of me, too."

My breath caught. If only he knew. "Uh...even if that was true, why would I admit that? No need to stroke your ego more," I teased.

He chuckled. "So your shower really wasn't lonely?" He asked again, almost sounding disappointed.

"Nope. Because I have two hands," I purred.

A noise came from the other end of the line that sounded like he had dropped the phone, making me giggle. There was a pause, and then he came back. "Now that is something that I would love to see."

I took a deep breath. "That could be arranged."

"God, you're fucking killing me, little one."

I thought a moment. There was intense mutual attraction between the two of us. It was only a matter of time before something happened. My body craved him and reacted to this man in a way I never thought was possible. "You do have my address, Sebastian."

"Shit, I'm on my way," he said, growling.

I laughed as the line disconnected. A moment of hesitation fluttered through me. This was it. Sebastian is coming over. Oh God.

He was a stranger. I knew nothing about the guy except that I was physically attracted to him. Would this be a one-night stand or would he want more? Shaking myself from those thoughts, I needed to keep busy and walked to my closet, searching for something to wear. Not being able to concentrate, I headed to my kitchen instead to make some coffee.

A hard knock sounded on my door, stopping me in my tracks.

He's here already? My heart thumped against my chest as I walked to the door. "Who is it?"

"Open the door, little one."

I grinned at the husky voice coming from the other side. Reaching the door, I opened it, keeping the chain lock in place.

Sebastian was panting, and his eyes hungrily travelled over my towel-clad body. "Fuck me. Do you always answer the door in just a towel?" he asked.

"Hi, Sebastian. I wasn't expecting you so soon, and no, I only answer it wearing a towel when I know a certain individual is coming over."

"Oh? Is that so? And who would that certain individual be, baby?"

I smiled, licking my lips. "Wouldn't you like to know?"

His eyes widened as he watched my tongue move across my mouth. "Fucking let me in, little one."

"Now why would I want to do that?" I teased.

"You know why." He pushed on the door, making it creak and strain against the lock.

"No, I don't." I took a step away from him when his hand grabbed my arm, pulling me towards him.

"I think you do know why."

"Yeah? Are you psychic now, Sebastian?" I grabbed onto his jacket.

He looked down at my lips. "No, but I know when a woman wants me, and I know you want me."

In one quick move, he had his hand behind my neck and his mouth on mine before I could even take a breath. His tongue moved against mine, as he continued to push on the door.

My hands grazed down his shirt and grabbed onto his belt, pulling him towards me. The opening between the wall and the door was small, but somehow, he was able to fit his arm through it to grab onto me.

"Shit." He groaned against my mouth. "I need you to let me in."

Hearing him beg made my stomach jump with glee, knowing that he didn't beg anyone, especially not for sex. I bet he had women throwing themselves at him. A twinge of jealousy swam through my stomach, and I shook myself, ridding my mind of that thought.

I smiled, released myself from his grasp, and jumped back just as his hand grazed my towel. "Tsk tsk. Now is that any way to treat a lady?" I panted.

"Stop being a tease."

I feigned shock. "Me? A tease? You kissed me first, remember? And who left whom standing alone in the alley?"

"It's called anticipation, baby. It made you want more, didn't it?" He growled.

He was right. I did want more. But I wasn't telling him that. I'd let him figure that out on his own. I shrugged. "I guess."

"You guess? Fuck, little one. Let me in right now, dammit."

I laughed and turned around, sauntering away from him. "Nope, you want it, you have to come and get it."

A hand hit the wall.

I turned to him, looking over my shoulder, and ran my hands up my body, slowly lifting the towel to my hips.

"Little one…" he said, his voice breathy. His eyes followed my hands running over my body.

As I hooked my fingers in the top of my towel, the door creaked more as Sebastian pushed on it. I turned again and let the towel fall off me, still holding it in one hand.

The door slammed open with a bang, and I shrieked, running to my bedroom.

"Oh, I don't fucking think so."

I laughed, making it to my room just in time, and quickly wrapped the towel back around me.

"Lose the towel," he demanded.

I ran around my bed as Sebastian entered my room. "Nope."

He dove across the bed, and I squealed, running back out the door. "There's nowhere for you to go," he called from behind me.

I ran into my kitchen, the island being the only thing separating us.

"You can't run into the hall naked."

"No? Try me."

His nostrils flared. "You better not."

"And why not?" I asked, backing up.

"Because your body is for my eyes only."

My cheeks heated at his words. What had he meant by that? Not having time to think about what he just said, I made a run for the door. My lungs were burning with excitement once I reached it. Wrapping my shaking hands around the knob, I got the door open part way when a hand slapped down and slammed it shut. My heart pounded harder at being caught, and my loins tingled with anticipation.

"You are the first woman to ever run away from me," he growled in my ear.

My heart thundered against my chest, and I could feel the heat coming off him in waves as he stood inches away from me.

"And I can't believe how fucking hard it made me." He grabbed the towel and ripped it off, leaving me standing naked against the door.

Hot breath grazed my ear and down my neck, sending shivers up my spine.

"Me chasing you." His fingers skimmed down my back to my ass and his hips ground into mine, pushing me up against the door.

I moaned as he lightly bit my shoulder. "Oh God."

"Oh, little one, God can't protect you now." He spun me around, and I gasped as he lifted me, throwing me over his shoulder.

"Let me down." I wiggled in his arms.

He hooked his arm around my legs and smacked my ass, making me squeal with delight. "Stop moving."

I continued to squirm and wiggle in his arms as I looked at the world upside down.

He smacked my ass again, and a moan escaped my lips. He chuckled. "Like that, do we?"

My body warmed but I didn't answer. I didn't need to.

As he walked me to my bedroom, a hand grazed up the back of my thighs.

I whimpered as a finger stroked over my wet core and slowly entered me.

"Oh yeah, you love being spanked, don't you?" Proving his point, he slapped my ass again and then rubbed gently over the tingling spot.

Moaning, I grabbed the back of his jacket. "More."

He slapped my ass on the other cheek, and I gasped, liquid heat roaring through my core. Reaching my bedroom, he laid me gently on the bed. His eyes darkened as he ran a finger up my core.

I moaned and arched under him.

"Oh, little one. I am going to fuck you like you've never been fucked before."

I panted. "Please."

"But, since you've had your fun, I think it's my turn now." He took off his leather jacket and threw it behind him. He ran his hands over the waist of his jeans and slowly brought his shirt over his head.

I licked my lips and couldn't help but stare at his big, hard body. Tattoos covered his torso, and both his nipples were pierced. He was gorgeous, and at the moment, he was all mine.

"Like what you see, little one?"

"Oh God, yes." I sat up and moved to my knees, kneeling before him. I rubbed a thumb over his bottom lip before covering his mouth with mine.

He grabbed the back of my neck and growled, forcing his tongue between my lips.

I moaned as our tongues danced, moving together. I released his mouth. "Sebastian, please…"

He trailed soft kisses down my jawline to my shoulder and over my breast.

I gasped as his mouth covered my nipple, pulling and sucking, and I cried out as teeth grazed the budding peak. My fingers ran through the hair at his nape, and my head fell back on my neck. I jumped as a finger touched my clit and panted as it entered me.

"Oh yeah, I could so get used to this."

I moaned in response.

He lifted his head from my nipple and looked down at me while he thrust his finger in me. "Do you like that?"

My body shuddered as waves of pleasure coursed through me. "Oh…my…God…yes…"

He chuckled. "Do you like my finger in your pussy?"

My knees shook as an orgasm quickly built up. "Yes." I moaned.

"Good, but as much as I want to feel you come against my hand, that's gonna have to wait."

I almost whimpered in disappointment.

"Oh, don't worry, little one. You'll come, but it'll be around my cock." He grabbed my chin and slammed his mouth down on mine, shoving his tongue in my mouth. With his other hand he lifted me, laying me back down on the bed.

Wiggling under him as he inserted his finger in me again, I arched under him and cried out as he stroked my clit. Positioning his hips between my legs, he removed his finger from me. Letting go of my chin, he rose on his knees.

I panted and watched him undo his jeans. The contours of his hard stomach dipped into hips that I wanted to sink my teeth into.

He pushed them down, revealing his hard cock that made me salivate. He was huge. Bigger than any other man I had ever been with, and I couldn't wait to feel him in me.

Licking my lips and wanting to taste the bead of liquid forming at the tip, I reached for him.

Grabbing my hands, he stopped me. "Little one, you keep looking at my cock like that, this won't last very long."

I looked up at him as his large hand wrapped around himself. He lowered his hand and moved it back up the shaft, covering the head.

Watching him touch himself was the sexiest thing I've ever seen, but that could wait. I needed him in me so badly that I ached for him. "Please." I lifted my hips, trying to move toward him so he could enter me.

Releasing himself, he placed his hands on my hips, turning me onto my side. The sound of a tin foil package opening sent a shiver down my spine.

I turned completely onto my stomach and rose on all fours and gasped when my feet were pulled out from under me. Spreading my knees apart, he kneeled between my legs.

"Little one," he growled into my ear. "You're going to take me deep, and you're going to love it aren't you?" He sheathed himself with a condom, keeping his fingers wrapped tight around the base.

I moaned as he teased my sex with the head of his cock. "Oh, yes…"

"Do you like that?" he asked, teasing me.

"Yes." I breathed. Shivers ran through my core at the way he handled my body like he knew exactly what I wanted and liked.

"Think you can handle me fucking you?"

My core pulsed at his words, and I arched under him. "Yes."

"Good, because I'm going to fuck you hard and fast, Tori."

CHAPTER NINE

MY CORE ACHED FOR him, and I moaned in response. I needed him. Wanted him from the first moment I had laid eyes on him. "Please…now. Stop teasing me."

"Why? What do you want?" Amusement coated his deep voice.

I arched up to him, ready to take him completely, but he held my waist, keeping me still. "I already told you want I wanted."

"Tell me again," he demanded, smoothing a hand down my hip.

Was he serious?

He continued to tease me with his cock, making me shiver. "Beg me."

"Sebastian."

"Beg me for it and I'll give you what you need, what you desire," he growled. He thrust his cock into me, but not filling me completely, and pulled back out.

I panted; sweat coated my skin as he continued to torture me. Oh God. "Please, fuck me. Now. I can't take this anymore. I need you."

"What do you want, little one?" he asked again, pulling me to the edge of the bed.

"I want you. Please, Sebastian," I pleaded.

"Oh, I know that already, baby. But what else do you want?" He rubbed the head of his cock over my core.

"I need you in me. Right… Oh, Sebastian!" I cried out as he thrust into me in one smooth move, filling me to the hilt.

"God, you feel good." He paused, letting my body get used to the fullness of him.

I panted and pushed back. "Please…" I panted. "…don't stop."

He chuckled and tightened his hold on my waist. "Hold on, baby."

He removed himself from me completely, and I cried out when he slammed back into my throbbing core. He continued to thrust in me, holding my hips.

I fisted the sheets in my hands, arching my hips to him as he drove into me.

"Oh, shit," he groaned. Grabbing onto my hair, he yanked my head back and covered my mouth with his. His hips moved faster, thrusting his cock in and out of me.

I spread my legs wider for him, opening myself to him as he continued to pound into me. "Ohh…Sebastian."

He groaned against my mouth, and I arched my hips, meeting him thrust for thrust, tingles spreading throughout my core.

Releasing his mouth, I screamed as an orgasm exploded from inside me. Aftershocks from the ecstasy shuddered through me as he continued his hard thrusts.

"Fuuuuuuck." A moment later, his body shook as his release erupted into me.

I sighed, deeply satisfied.

Resting his elbows on either side of my head, he placed a soft kiss on my shoulder. "That was fucking incredible."

I moaned and clenched around him, enjoying the feel of him still in me. "Oh, yes, it was."

He jumped. "You don't want to do that."

I smiled and clenched again. "And why not?" Moving my hips, I felt him slowly harden inside me.

"Shit, little one."

I laughed.

"Two can play at this game." Removing himself from me, he turned me onto my back.

I gasped as he started rubbing my clit. Squeezing the sheets in my hands, I closed my eyes and moaned.

He rubbed my clit harder and faster with his thumb as two fingers entered me.

Arching under him, I squeezed my eyes shut. My clit was still sensitive, but as he continued to flick the swollen nub, fire brewed deep within me. Another orgasm started from my toes and quickly spread up through my body.

Rising on all fours, he continued to rub the throbbing nub and licked the crook of my neck. Sebastian bit my shoulder, and my scream sounded around the room as another orgasm shattered my insides. Grabbing my jaw, he covered my mouth and swallowed the rest of my scream. "God, I fucking love the sounds you make when you come."

I whimpered.

Placing one last kiss on my lips, he hopped off the bed. "You're so beautiful."

My face heated.

"And your blush definitely goes all the way down."

I smiled. My muscles ached and were sore in places that hadn't been used in a while. It was wonderful. I lay there watching Sebastian undress completely. The muscles moved fluidly over his abdomen, and I tried not to drool.

He grabbed the blanket that was folded on the end of my bed and placed it over me.

"What are you doing?" I asked him.

"I am joining you for a nap."

I frowned. "Why? What time is it?"

"It's only ten a.m."

"Oh."

Lying down beside me, he brought the blanket over us both. "Why? Got a big date planned today?"

I laughed. "Um...no." As he pulled me against him, I remembered the good news I got today. "Oh, I did get a job, though."

"That's wonderful, little one." he said.

"It's just doing office stuff but it's nine-to-five, so I can't complain," I explained. I turned to him, and he was smiling down at me.

"A job is a job, baby. It helps pay the bills. I'm proud of you." He ran a hand down my cheek, making my heart flutter.

I smiled. "I'm happy."

"That's good." He kissed my nose. "Now get some sleep."

"I'm not tired." Just as those words left my lips, a huge yawn bubbled up from inside me.

He chuckled and kissed my forehead. "Get some sleep 'cause I plan on doing some more of this..."

I gasped when his finger grazed over my core and entered me slowly.

"...when we wake up." Sebastian continued thrusting his finger in and out of me slowly, waking up my body again.

I closed my eyes, enjoying the feel of him pleasuring my body when he removed his finger from me, leaving me empty with need. "You didn't have to stop."

"Why? Do you like it when I fuck you with my fingers?" Moving his hand down to my pussy, he thrust two fingers into me hard, making me cry out.

"Sebastian."

"Come again for me," he said, speeding up his fingers. Kissing my shoulder, his gaze bored into mine, watching me come undone beside him.

Another orgasm erupted from my middle, and I shook and quaked against his hand. "Oh…my…"

Biting my shoulder, he removed his hand from me. "Now, get some sleep, baby, because we are doing that again when we wake up."

Licking my lips, I took a deep breath, easing my racing heart from the multiple orgasms.

"Would you like that, little one?" He ran a hand down my side, making me shiver.

I pressed into him and sighed. "Oh, yes."

"Would you like it if I fucked you every chance I got?" he whispered against my ear.

"Oh God, yes."

He smirked and pulled me to him, wrapping his arms around me. "Good, 'cause little one, I don't plan on leaving anytime soon."

His legs curled around mine, and he placed a kiss on my shoulder. I sighed and fell asleep to his hand soothingly running over my hip.

***

Stirring awake, I rolled over. With my eyes still closed, I ran a hand over the spot beside me and frowned when I realized it was empty.

I opened my eyes and turned onto my back. Sighing, I sat up and groaned, my muscles hurting and twitching in all the right places. Smiling to myself, I removed the covers and headed to the bathroom. As I approached the closed door, I heard Sebastian talking to someone.

"Listen, asshole…"

I frowned, placing my hand on the doorknob.

"No, I won't stay away from her."

Was he talking about me?

"You can't tell me what to do. I don't care who you are… No, Jose hasn't called me."

If he wasn't talking to Jose, then who was he talking to?

"He called her? No, I had no idea."

Oh, shit.

"Whatever, asshole. I'm sure she'll tell me. Hey, you watch what you say about… Fuck you… You can go to hell."

I jumped as something hit the door. A moment later, the shower started running.

I tentatively opened the door and walked into the bathroom. Slowly closing it behind me, I leaned against the door. I could see Sebastian's large form behind the clear curtain. The air became thick with condensation, and I headed to the shower. I pulled back the curtain and stepped into the tub behind him.

His beautiful back was to me, hard and strong. Tattoos roamed down his naked torso, and scars marred his skin. What happened to him?

I stepped up to him and placed my hand on his back, gently running my fingers over the raised flesh. He tensed at first under my touch.

I placed my other hand on his arm.

He reached over and grabbed it, bringing it to his lips, kissing my knuckles.

I leaned into him, resting my head against his back, letting the water wash over me.

"Jose called you."

I sighed. "Yeah, he did. I meant to tell you. I'm so sorry."

He rose to his full height and turned around, facing me.

I looked up into his dark eyes. "Sebastian…"

"You don't need to apologize. Just…" He placed a hand on my cheek, and I leaned into it. "Just next time, tell me."

"But…"

"Little one, trust me. You don't know who you're dealing with."

"Okay. Who was on the phone?"

Surprise marked his features, and then he hid it by grabbing the shampoo. "No one important."

"Okay, but…"

He paused before bringing his hands to his hair. "Little one, just drop it."

"Fine." I turned and pulled back the curtain.

"Where are you going?"

I looked back at him, trying not to stare at the soap running down his hard chest and abs.

"You don't have to leave," he added.

I chewed on my bottom lip. "I…I just feel like you're keeping something from me, and I'm really dumb for saying that 'cause it's not like I'm your girlfriend or anything, but I guess…I guess I just worry for you." I took a deep breath.

His eyes searched my face, and he took a step toward me. Pinching my chin, he ran his thumb over my bottom lip. "You're worried for me?"

I rolled my eyes and huffed. "Yes, all right? Jose scares the shit out of me, and I don't know who the hell was on the phone, but whoever it was, I seriously want to kick his ass for making you mad and ruining the mood."

Sebastian chuckled lightly. "Oh, little one, he didn't ruin the mood." He placed a soft kiss on my lips.

I sighed against his mouth.

He looked down at me. "But there are things that I can't tell you, and I need you to be patient with me. Also, you are not fucking dumb, so don't ever say that."

"Sebastian, I…"

"Please." His eyes pleaded with me.

"Fine, I'll be patient. I'm sorry for being such a…"

His mouth slammed on mine, tongue diving between my lips. He grabbed my hands and pushed me up against the shower wall and lifted me. "Condom," he breathed.

"I'm on the pill," I said softly.

He leaned back, a smug smile forming on his handsome face.

I smiled back. Gripping his arms, I trailed my fingers over his tattoos before cupping the back of his neck.

He smirked and crashed his mouth to mine. Forcing his tongue between my lips, he pushed my knees up to my chest at the same time he entered me.

I whimpered, tightening my thighs around him as he continued to thrust into me.

He held onto my hips, quickening his movements. His mouth moved from my lips down to my neck.

Placing my hands on his shoulders, I squeezed and dug my fingers into his hard flesh.

His head rested on my shoulder, his breathing coming out in short gasps. Lifting me up and down on his cock, he fucked me against the cool tiled wall.

"Oh, Sebastian." I cried out as an orgasm shook from my middle. Scratching his back, I slammed my head against the wall as the intense explosion bubbled up from my core.

I wrapped my hands around his neck and moaned when he shuddered against me, having his own release. "Fuck, little one." He moaned, slowing his hips.

"Um...thank you?"

He chuckled and looked down at me. "I think I should be thanking you."

My cheeks warmed, and I smiled up at him.

He placed me on my feet and continued his shower.

I leaned against the wall and licked my lips, watching him.

He paused. "You need to stop looking at me like that."

I giggled. "Why?"

He grabbed my hand and pulled me to him, placing it on his already semi-hard cock.

My eyes widened. He was bigger than I had thought.

"That's..." His breath hitched as I moved my hand, wrapping it around him.

I kissed his chest as I lowered my hand around his cock. Moving to his nipple, I took the bud into my mouth and ran my tongue around the metal barbell.

A deep groan came from the back of his throat as his hand moved to my nape, fisting my hair between his fingers.

I ran my thumb over the head of his cock and gasped when he tugged my hair back, forcing me to look up at him.

"Little one, think you can handle me fucking you again?" he asked in a husky voice.

Licking my lips, I moaned. "Oh, yes."

***

An hour later we finally emerged from the shower, both satiated and satisfied.

As Sebastian got dressed, I ran lotion over my legs. "I never thought that a woman rubbing lotion on herself would be hot as hell."

I giggled and slowly ran my hands back down my legs, spreading the lotion on myself. Never before would I have thought that I would be standing in my room in just my bra and panties with the most gorgeous man watching me.

"God, you're gonna be the death of me."

I held out the lotion bottle and looked up at him innocently. "Can you lotion my back, please?"

His eyes blazed, but then he shook his head. "Nope, I can't."

I pouted.

He chuckled and took a step toward me. Placing a soft kiss on my lips, he leaned down to my ear and cupped my ass. "If I start rubbing lotion on your back, then I will never leave." He ran a tongue up my ear, igniting shivers in my back.

"And that's a bad thing because?" I purred.

He laughed. "It's not a bad thing, trust me, but do you really want to spend the day inside?"

"Uh…if we do what we've been doing for the last couple of hours, then yes."

He laughed and shook his head. "You're worse than a guy."

I smacked his arm. "Well, it's your fault, you know."

He feigned shock. "My fault?"

"Um…yeah. If you 'hadn't kissed me in the alley…"

Sebastian placed a kiss on my shoulder. "Yeah?"

I swallowed. "Then I…"

"Then you what?" he asked, trailing kisses up my neck.

"I wouldn't have just had the best sex of my life," I quickly blurted.

He lifted his head, a smug grin spread on his face, and he pulled me into an embrace. "Oh, yes you would have."

I frowned and looked up at him, wrapping my hands around his waist. "Really?"

He grabbed my chin and brushed his lips over mine. "I wouldn't have been able to stay away from you, little one. Even if I 'hadn't um…grabbed you in the alley, I would have found some way to get your attention."

"Well, you definitely got my attention." I ran my hands up his back.

"That was the goal, baby. But best sex, huh?"

I sighed. "Oh, hell, yeah."

He laughed. Squeezing my ass, he pulled me against him.

"Oh, shit." I gasped, remembering that I'd forgotten to call Keisha, and released myself from his grip.

"What's wrong?"

"I have to call Keisha." I ran to my phone and turned on the screen. Five text messages and two missed calls. I dialed her number. I hoped she wasn't working today.

She answered a couple of rings later. "Tori, where the hell are you?"

"Keisha." I sat on my bed. "I'm at home. How are you feeling?"

"Ugh, like shit. I'm never drinking tequila again."

I laughed. "I think we've all been there."

Sebastian moved to the window and leaned against the wall, watching me.

I placed the phone on the desk, turning on the speaker. "'K, you're on speaker phone now so I can finish getting dressed."

"Okay, so are you coming to the coffee shop today?"

"Are you working?" I pulled on jeans and threw on a T-shirt, all the while trying very hard to ignore Sebastian's heated scrutiny.

"Yeah, I got called in."

I felt for her. "Tell them you're sick."

Warm arms wrapped around me as Sebastian pulled me against him. "Tell her you have to go," he whispered in my ear.

"They know I went out last night," Keisha continued.

My breath hitched when his hips ground against mine, his erection pressing against my ass. He was ready to go again so soon? Knowing that I did that to him made liquid pool in my panties. "Oh, well…"

Ringing came from the bathroom. "Shit."

"What was that?" Keisha asked.

"It's another cell phone," I said.

Sebastian sighed, releasing me. "I thought I broke it."

"Who was that?"

"Hello, Keisha." He called as he headed into the bathroom.

"Was that Sebastian?"

I coughed, my face heating. "Um…yes."

"What the he—"

I quickly took her off speaker phone. "Keisha."

"No, I'm not judging. I'm just surprised," she quickly said.

"Really?" It wasn't that big of a surprise that he was at my place, was it?

Keisha laughed. "Okay, maybe not that surprised but still. Why didn't you tell me?"

"Well, it kinda just happened." And I hoped that it would happen again and again and…

Sebastian came out of the bathroom looking distraught.

"Keisha, I have to go." Something was wrong.

"What? Why? I want details."

"I'll see you in a bit," I told her. I hung up and walked toward Sebastian. "What's wrong?"

He placed his hands in his pockets. "I have to go."

My heart sped up. "Okay."

"I'll meet you at the coffee shop. If I'm not with you and you see Jose, I want you to leave right away. Don't stay around him. Okay?" he said, grabbing his jacket.

"Sebastian…"

"Okay?" His voice was desperate.

"Okay," I whispered.

He nodded, seeming satisfied with my response, and placed a quick kiss on my lips and turned. Once he reached my door, he looked back at me and sighed.

I took a step toward him. He walked back to me and met me halfway, his lips finding mine.

"Don't leave yet," I said against his mouth.

His hands grabbed my ass and lifted me.

I hooked my hands around his neck and wrapped my legs around his waist.

"God, little one."

I covered his mouth and plunged my tongue between his lips. My pussy throbbed and ached to be touched by him again. I couldn't get enough of this man. My body hummed for him, tingles igniting all over me.

His tongue danced with mine as he dug his fingers into my ass cheeks, pulling me toward him.

I gasped when we hit the wall, not realizing that we had moved.

He lifted his head. "I have to go." He moved his pelvis against mine.

I licked his bottom lip, enjoying the feel of his erection against my core. "Yeah, I know." His breath hitched as I sucked and pulled at his lip.

"But I don't want to." His voice came out husky.

"I don't want you to, either." I ran my hands up under the front of his shirt, my fingers grazing his hard stomach. He leaned his forehead against mine, his breathing heavy. "I really should go, baby."

"I think whoever you were talking to can wait," I said as I reached between us. Cupping his thick cock over his jeans, I rubbed lightly, making him jump.

His hands tightened on my ass. "God, you feel good."

I smiled. "I can feel better, too." Unbuckling his belt, I lowered his zipper and reached into his pants, smiling that he was going commando. I wrapped my hand around his hard cock, releasing it from his jeans.

His breath hitched, and he lifted his head from mine, his eyes blazing. "I love it when a woman knows what she wants."

I smirked. "I want you, and I would feel better if my pussy was wrapped around your cock," I replied, squeezing his erection hard.

His hips bucked against my hand. "You want me again?"

"Oh, please, yes." I think I'd always want him.

He backed up and placed me on my feet.

I was about to ask what he was doing when he lowered his jeans completely, springing free his erection. He grabbed it in one large hand, gripping it tight.

My nostrils flared, and I licked my lips at the sight.

Sebastian cleared his throat.

I looked up at him, and he motioned at my jeans. I quickly clued in, undid the button, and had them off just as he pushed me up against the wall.

Lifting me, he wrapped my legs around his hips and lowered me onto him. We both groaned at the same time. "Hold on, little one."

Tightening my legs around him, I held onto his shoulders. I gasped, crying out as he held me against the wall and thrust in and out of me. I stayed still and let him have his way with my body, pleasuring both of us and bringing us to pure ecstasy. "Sebastian," I screamed.

He grunted, squeezing my hips as he pounded into my aching core. "God, you feel so good."

I moaned, digging my heels into his ass. An orgasm slowly built, starting from my toes as he pumped into me faster and faster against the wall.

He groaned, lifted me completely off him, and lowered me in one smooth thrust back onto his cock, pushing my orgasm forward full force. I screamed his name over and over as he thrust into me hard and fast.

He stopped and thrust into me one last time, his body shaking as he climaxed, releasing into me. Placing a hard kiss on my lips, he slowly let me down. "I could do that all day."

I moaned and wrapped my hands around his neck. "Me too."

He sighed and kissed me one last time. "But I really do have to go now."

Righting himself, he watched me get dressed.

Doing up my jeans, I walked him to the door.

He turned back to me before leaving. "Remember what I said." He paused. "I'll make sure to fix your door."

I nodded, smiling. A flutter of disappointment flowed through me as he shut the door behind him. I was falling for Sebastian quickly.

He asked me to be patient with him, and I would, but what if patience wasn't enough?

CHAPTER TEN

I **FINISHED GETTING READY** after Sebastian left my apartment, then I headed to the coffee shop about an hour later. It being early afternoon, the place wasn't that busy.

Keisha was fluttering about, wiping off tables as I entered. I approached her, and she looked up at me, smiling. "Have a good morning?" She winked.

My face heated. "I don't think good is the right word for it."

She laughed. "What word would you use to describe it then?"

I thought a moment, grinning. "How about fucking incredible?"

"That's two words."

I shrugged. It was incredible, and I had the sore muscles to prove it. "It definitely deserves two words."

She laughed again, walking to the counter. "Your usual?"

"Yes, please." I sat down on the couch and pulled out my book from my bag.

"Hey, fancy meeting you here."

I looked up and saw Brett standing in front of me. He wore a white button-up shirt, sleeves rolled up to his elbows, and black dress pants. I wondered if he ever dressed casually.

I noticed a shadow of scruff on his jaw, which enhanced his good looks, but he was no Sebastian. "Hi."

"Mind if I join you?"

"That depends."

His face hardened. "On what?"

"You going to give me issues about being friends with Keisha?"

He looked back at Keisha and then at me. "No."

"Good. Then yes, you can join me."

He sat across from me, and my gaze met Keisha's. A look of concern marked her features. Turning back to Brett, I leaned back in my seat. "You didn't tell Keisha about our little argument this morning, did you?"

He crossed his arms under his chest. "No. I didn't."

I nodded. "I didn't think so."

Brett sighed. "Tori, listen…"

I held up my hand. "No, it's fine. I understand. You're her big brother, and you have every right to protect her."

"There are some things you don't know."

I laughed. "Wow. I'm getting told that a lot today."

He frowned. "Who else told you that?"

"It doesn't matter." I placed my book down beside me. I was getting sick and tired of being left in the dark.

"Are you two getting along?" Keisha asked as she walked up to us, placing two coffees on the table.

I looked at Brett.

His jaw tightened. "Yeah, we're getting along just fine. We were just talking about going out to dinner."

My eyes widened. He wanted to go out to dinner with me? I couldn't do that after spending the morning with Sebastian. That wouldn't be right. "Brett, I don't…"

"Really?" Keisha looked at me, suspicion coating her features. "Are you sure that's a good idea?"

She probably thought I was a slut who wanted Sebastian and her brother. I looked back at Brett. "Brett…"

"Just as friends," he clarified.

Grinding my teeth together, I put on a fake smile for Keisha. "Yes, apparently we're going as friends."

He smirked.

Asshole.

"Okay…well…good then, I guess. Just be careful, Tor."

I smiled up at Keisha in reassurance. When she left, I turned back to Brett. "Really? Dinner?"

He chuckled. "I like you, and dinner was the first thing that popped into my head."

I sighed. What was with these men who thought they could get whatever they wanted whenever they wanted? "Brett…"

"There's nothing wrong with dinner. It's not like you and Sebastian are serious."

Thank you for the reminder. I rolled my eyes. "Does Keisha know what's going on?"

"What do you mean?"

"You told me there are some things that I don't know."

He scowled. "Of course she doesn't know."

"Well how do you expect to protect her if she doesn't know what she needs to be protected from?"

He huffed. "That's the point. If she doesn't know anything, I can protect her more."

I scoffed. "Yeah, 'cause that always works. She's gonna be pissed that you've been keeping stuff from her."

"Like you are that Sebastian's keeping things from you?"

My eyes widened. "How the fu—"

"Well, isn't this a happy couple?"

I turned to the voice that made my skin crawl and saw Jose walking around the couch. He sat beside Brett, smiling.

Oh, I so wanted to punch that slimy grin off his face. His pockmarks were more pronounced in the light of the coffee shop, and they made him seem scarier. Nervous butterflies flew through my belly. "What do you want, Jose?"

"Why, Brett, I just came here for a coffee. No harm in that, right?" He smirked and leaned back on the couch, placing an ankle on his opposite knee.

I chewed my bottom lip as I contemplated leaving, knowing that I should probably head home since that was what Sebastian had told me to do.

"What's wrong, Tori?" Jose winked at me. A dark bruise covered his jaw from when Sebastian hit him last night, and I smiled to myself.

I cleared my throat, grabbing my stuff. "I should…" I looked up just as Sebastian sat down beside me. A moment of relief flooded through me, and I let out a deep breath.

His body was tense, and he clenched his jaw.

I turned to him, curling a leg under me. "Sebastian."

He lightly shook his head and took a deep breath. Placing a hand on my knee, he rubbed his thumb back and forth.

I frowned, anxiety swirling around in my belly. "What's…"

"So I see you've made a new friend in my partner," Jose pointed out, nodding his chin toward Sebastian.

My gaze snapped to Jose. He was looking down at Sebastian's hand on my knee. Jose glanced at Sebastian, anger flashing in his eyes, and then looked back at me.

"Yeah, well, from what I understand, partner isn't the correct term," I bit out.

Jose smirked and turned to Brett. "So, Brett, how's the business?"

I turned to Sebastian, placing my hand on his arm. "Sebastian," I whispered.

"Not now, little one." His voice was deep and laced with concern.

"Look at me," I pleaded.

His head slowly turned to face me.

I gasped at the fury and rage dancing in his eyes.

"Tori," Jose said.

I turned to him. "What?" I snapped.

An evil glint flashed in Jose's black eyes, and his lips turned up. Jaw clenching, his gaze bored into mine. "I think I like her, but you definitely got your hands full with this one, Sebastian." He laughed and leaned back in his seat.

Sebastian squeezed my knee. "Don't I know it."

My gazed eyes flashed to his. "What the hell is going on, Sebastian?"

"We'll talk later," he said quietly.

"Sebastian." I was sick of his secrets. I didn't really have any right to demand he talk to me, but he had spent all morning in my bed, so I felt an explanation of some kind was in order.

His head snapped around, eyes furious. "I said, drop it."

Anger burned in my belly, and I pushed his hand off my knee. Crossing my legs, I folded my arms across my chest.

Jose laughed. "Ah, I think someone is getting suspicious."

I glared at him and turned away, ignoring the looks of I told you so that Brett was giving me.

Sebastian placed his hand back on my knee, and I pushed it off again.

He grabbed my hand and laced his fingers in mine.

I tried prying my hand out of his, but he squeezed it, pulling me towards him. "Stop it."

I glared at him. "Let go of me."

He growled. "No."

"I said, let go of me." Pushing away from him, I attempted to rise from the couch.

"And I said no. Now stop making a scene."

I huffed and ignored the looks from customers at the tables around us, not caring in the slightest if they saw what an asshole Sebastian was being at the moment. "What the hell happened, Sebastian?"

"Patience, little one," he said quietly.

"You don't know me at all, do you?"

His gaze flicked to mine. "What do you mean?"

I rolled my eyes. "Patience is something I do not have."

"Oh, I know baby, trust me, but you need to start trying." He turned back to Jose, tightly holding my hand.

"Asshole," I mumbled.

A light chuckle came from Sebastian.

Sighing, I crossed my legs under me and placed our joined hands in my lap. If I wasn't allowed to leave, I was at least going to get comfortable.

I promised I would be patient, or try to be anyway, but the change in his mood since this morning really pissed me off. Something had happened since he left my apartment a couple of hours ago, and I knew it had to do with Jose.

"So, Sebastian. You mind if I take your girl out for dinner?"

My gaze snapped to Brett's as Sebastian tensed beside me.

"Why would you take Tori out to dinner?" Sebastian bit out.

I watched as Jose's eyes flicked between the two of them. "Oh, this is gonna get fucking good."

"Well, Tori did agree to go out to dinner with me," Brett said like it was no big deal.

Sebastian's hand tightened around mine, making me wince.

"I didn't really have a choice in the matter." I glared at Brett.

"You always have a choice." Sebastian said with a growl.

I sighed. "No, I didn't," I argued. Could this day get any worse?

Sebastian lowered his lips to my ear. "He just better remember that you're mine."

My heart skipped a beat at his words. "What does that mean?" I whispered.

He grabbed my chin, his hot breath on my ear. "I don't share, and I definitely don't play nice with pretty boys." He licked my ear.

Shivers ran up my spine. "I don't want him."

He looked down into my eyes, his gaze heating. "Good."

"Don't worry, Sebastian. I won't touch her. She made it quite clear that we're just going as friends," Brett stated.

Sebastian lifted his head and glared at Brett.

Brett and Jose smiled at each other and then turned back to me.

Something told me that they got along better than they let on, and I had a feeling that they were setting Sebastian up, but then something occurred to me. "Brett, I thought you didn't like Jose."

Brett tensed and shifted in his seat but didn't respond.

"Sebastian?" I said quietly.

"Yeah."

"I thought they didn't get along." I was confused. I had no idea what was going on. Brett had warned me to stay away from Jose and Sebastian, but Brett was the one who was confusing me the most.

"I'm not sure, baby," he said, running his thumb over the back of my hand.

"What's the big deal whether we go on a date or not, anyway?" Brett asked.

"It's not a date, Brett," I corrected.

"You'd better not touch her, or I'll break every bone in your body and make you wish you were fucking dead. You'll beg me to kill you," Sebastian warned.

I gasped at his words, looking between him and Brett.

Amusement coated Brett's features as if he was trying to piss Sebastian off. "If I touch her, you won't know about it, asshole."

Before I even had a chance to respond, Sebastian was on his feet, his face inches from Brett's. "Yeah? You think so, do you? Remember who she chose first."

I watched him as he walked to the hall leading to the washrooms.

Brett and Jose chuckled as I followed him.

"Sebastian," I called after him.

He spun on me, forcing me to take a step back.

Before I knew what was happening, he was on me, pushing me up against the wall. His mouth covered mine, forcing his tongue between my lips. His fingers dug into my shoulders as he deepened the kiss. Like he was marking me. As his. Owning me. Possessing me. Letting everyone, including me, know that I was his.

Butterflies flew around in my stomach at this thought, but I grabbed onto his waist, pulling him against me.

He groaned into my mouth and then released me, resting his forehead against mine, his chest heaving.

I closed my eyes, panting. Running my hands inside his jacket, I wrapped my arms around him. "Sebastian. You need to talk to me."

He sighed, lightly grazing his fingers down my cheek. "Please be careful around those guys. I don't fucking trust them."

"Brett said the same thing about you pretty much."

He looked down at me. "Do you trust me?"

"Of course," I responded with no hesitation.

A small smile tugged at his lips. "Good, I'm glad."

I smiled up at him. "I will be careful though, I promise."

He placed a soft kiss on my lips. "I'm gonna drag Jose's ass out of here. I'll call you soon, little one."

I nodded and leaned against the wall, watching him head back to Jose and Brett. Keisha rounded the corner, looking behind her and then at me. "What the hell is going on?"

I sighed. "I really wish I knew."

CHAPTER ELEVEN

A WEEK HAD PASSED since I'd heard from Sebastian. Every time my phone rang, butterflies flew around in my stomach and then I was filled with disappointment when it wasn't him on the other end. Worry took up permanent residence in my heart, and my chest ached for him.

I had started my new job, so I kept myself busy with learning the ins and outs of that. It was easy mindless work but I enjoyed it.

The weekend finally came, bringing along with it the preemptive night out with Brett. It made my stomach clench with uneasiness at the thought of going out to dinner with another man.

As I was getting ready, my phone rang. I quickly ran to it and answered, hope rising that it was Sebastian. "Hello?"

"Hello, little one."

I breathed a sigh of relief. Hearing his voice as it washed over me eased some of the anxiety that had built up in my stomach. It felt odd being so attracted to a man when I hardly knew him, but he was a part of me. "Sebastian."

He lightly chuckled. "The one and only."

I giggled. "Where are you?"

He sighed. "I'm around."

"Is everything okay?" My heart sped up in my chest at the thought that something was wrong.

A moment passed before he responded. "Everything is fine, baby."

He was lying. "Sebastian…"

"Listen, the next time you see me, if I'm not acting myself, just trust me. All right? Remember to trust me."

"Sebastian, you're scaring me."

"I know."

He tried to make small talk with me. He remembered that I had started my new job the week before, and he seemed genuinely interested in my success. But I was distracted. I couldn't shake the feeling that something was going to happen or that he was in trouble. "Stop trying to change the subject."

"I'm so sorry, baby."

"What the hell are you talking about?" Panic rose in my voice at his words.

"I should go. I just wanted to hear your voice. I'll see you soon, little one, I promise."

"Wait. Sebastian? Come over. I can cancel my plans."

"No. Go enjoy your dinner, and I'll call you later to see if you're home from your night out with Brett." He growled the name.

"Okay. I'll see you later, then?" I rolled my eyes at the desperation in my voice.

"I don't know, maybe." His voice sounded sad.

"Well, can I call you at least?"

"You can only text me at the phone number I programmed into your phone, and then I'll call you back when I can."

My heart thudded against my chest. "Okay."

"Little one…"

"I'm just worried…" I sat down on the edge of my bed.

"I know, baby."

I sighed as the line disconnected.

***

An hour later, Brett picked me up. When I entered his car, his eyes were warm as he smiled at me. "How was your week?"

I turned to him and sighed. "It was all right. How was yours?"

"It was good. Something wrong, Tori?"

I frowned. "No, now why would something be wrong?"

He sighed. "I'm sorry for being an asshole the other day."

"Yeah, well, you kind of threw this date thing in Sebastian's face," I mumbled, not knowing what his issue was. He was nice the one moment and then he was off-putting. Did he really want to be friends or not?

"I know, and I'm sorry for that. I wish I could explain…"

"What?" I prodded when he didn't finish his sentence.

"Nothing. Forget I said anything."

"Brett."

"Tori."

I rolled my eyes and crossed my arms over my chest. Maybe I should have just stayed home.

"I know you didn't want to go out to dinner with me, but try and enjoy yourself," he grumbled.

"It's not that I don't want to go out to dinner with you. I just wish you would have asked me instead of telling me. I didn't appreciate you assuming I would go out with you."

"Then why did you agree?"

I shrugged. "I don't know…to shut you up, I guess."

He laughed. "Well I appreciate your honesty at least."

I smiled, looking out the window, watching the city fly by us. About ten minutes later, we reached the restaurant. It was a cute little Italian bistro, and my stomach rumbled at the thought of pasta. After we parked, Brett paused before he got out of the car. "Brett, I…"

He moved quickly and placed his mouth on mine, hand cupping my neck. It was a light kiss; his lips were warm and soft and he kept his tongue to himself. His skin was clean-shaven, so no scruff scratched at my cheeks, but he wasn't the man I wanted.

I placed my hands on his chest, pushing him.

He released my mouth and ran a hand over his hair. "I'm sorry. I shouldn't have done that. I'm such an asshole."

"No, you're not an asshole. It's fine. I'm not mad at you. Maybe it was a little untimely, but it's okay. Shit happens." I placed my hand on his arm.

He turned to me, his usual twinkle reappearing back in his eyes. "I love your colorful language."

I laughed. "Let's go have dinner."

"I am sorry, baby girl. I shouldn't have kissed you, especially when you have a thing going on with Sebastian. That was a dick move on my part."

I sighed. "No, you shouldn't have kissed me but whatever. It's done. Just please don't do it again."

He nodded. After getting out of the car, he walked around to my side and opened the door. "After you milady."

I giggled and stepped out of the vehicle.

He held his arm out to me, and I grabbed it, walking with him to the entrance.

My phone dinged and I reached into my clutch. As I checked it, I heard someone cough nearby.

"Well, well, well, now what do we have here?"

Brett stopped, forcing me to stop with him, and I looked up.

My stomach dropped as I saw three very tough looking guys surround us. My heart sped up. "Brett," I whispered.

He placed his other hand on mine, tightening it. "Hello, gentlemen. Nice evening, isn't it?"

The three guys looked at each other and laughed. "Yeah, it is a nice evening."

Unease settled in my belly as I recognized the voice. A fourth guy stepped from behind a van. It was Jose. "Brett, we should leave. Like right now. We can have dinner at my place." I took a step back.

"Yeah, Brett, you should listen to Tori." Jose sneered, taking a step towards us.

"What the hell do you want, Jose?" I bit out.

"Does Sebastian know you're out with Brett?" He smirked.

"Obviously. You were there when we were talking about it."

Jose glared at me but he didn't respond. "I spent time with your sister today, Brett. She sure is a pretty thing."

Brett took a step forward at the mention of his sister. I held onto his arm firmly. There was no way he would be able to take on four guys, and I definitely wouldn't be much help unless I gouged an eye out with my heel.

"Brett, don't."

"I'd listen to your girlfriend if I were you. Oh, wait, she isn't your girlfriend. I forgot, you're her second choice," Jose mocked as he took a step toward us.

I could feel the tension boiling off Brett as Jose got closer to us. We really needed to leave. I didn't know what would happen, but I didn't trust any of the guys in front of us.

"What do you want?"

Jose's gaze flashed to mine and then roamed over my body.

"You should never ask a deranged psychopath what they want." Sebastian came up behind Jose and clapped him on the shoulder, smirking at me. Jose laughed in agreement.

Shock flowed through me at seeing Sebastian there. "Sebastian, what the hell are you doing here?" And why was he all of a sudden chummy with Jose?

"Oh, I decided to join the fun." He turned to the other three guys. "You can leave."

Turning back to us, he stood beside Jose.

"You motherfucker cock-sucking piece of…"

Sebastian laughed, interrupting Brett's name-calling.

I pulled Brett's arm. "Let's go," I whispered. I didn't want to stay to find out exactly what they were doing here. We started backing up.

"I don't think so. Brett can leave, but you're not going anywhere, little one."

My stomach fell to my feet, and I spun on them.

"What do you want with her? You already got your piece."

"Brett." He turned to me, and I scowled at him.

"Yeah, and then she goes out with you after—kind of a slut move on her part." Jose glared at me.

Sebastian and Brett both turned to him. "Hey," they said at the same time, and they frowned at each other. Sebastian smacked Jose across the back of the head.

"Ow. I'm just saying." He rubbed his head.

Not really knowing why I should defend myself, I did it anyways. "Brett and I were just going to dinner as friends. Sebastian knew that."

"You're very lucky it wasn't me you fucked, because I wouldn't let you get away with going out with another guy. You could say, I'm kind of possessive that way."

Sebastian's head whipped to look at Jose, and he glared at him. "What happens between me and Tori is none of your fucking business, Jose."

Jose glared back at him, his fists clenching and unclenching.

"Yeah, well, it wasn't you, now, was it, so who cares what you think, asshole?" Apparently my filter was broken at this point because the look Jose gave me made me really regret those words that came out of my mouth.

Jose's head snapped my way, and he took a step toward me. "Watch it, cochina." Venom oozed from his voice.

Sebastian grabbed Jose behind the neck and whispered something in his ear, all the while Jose wouldn't turn his black eyes away from me.

"I think you're letting her get to you," he said quietly.

I frowned, confused.

"Don't worry about it. I got this." Sebastian looked at me. He walked up to me, and Brett tensed. Ignoring him, Sebastian grabbed my face with both hands and placed a hard kiss on my lips.

He leaned down to my ear. "Do you trust me?" he whispered.

"Sebastian. I…"

"Do you trust me?" he demanded.

"Yes, yes, of course, but you being here… It's confusing me…" My heart pounded against my chest. I didn't know what was going on, but seeing Sebastian with Jose and acting like they were friends really threw me off.

Sebastian brushed his lips against mine. "I know, baby. But I need you to fucking continue trusting me no matter what happens."

"I…What do you…"

He kissed me again and turned to Brett. "I don't like you, and I don't fucking trust you."

Brett scowled. "Feeling's mutual, asshole."

Sebastian smiled. "But I need you to watch out for Tori."

My eyebrows rose in confusion. "Sebastian, you said…"

His head snapped to mine. "I know what I said." Looking back at Brett, he asked again. "Will you watch out for her?"

"Of course." Brett answered.

"Sebastian." I grabbed his hand. "Just take me home, or we can go to Keisha's…"

"I'm sorry, baby." He placed another kiss on my lips and headed back in the direction he came from.

I watched him go, and a moment later my cell phone dinged. I checked it and read Stop staring at my ass. I blushed just as another text came through. I'll be seeing you soon, little one, and remember, trust me.

My heart fluttered. Taking a deep breath, I turned to Brett. "Let's go."

Jose still stood in front of me, eyes blazing, setting my nerves on edge. "Give us a second."

Brett looked between the two of us, and I nodded. "It's fine."

He started walking toward his car, making sure to keep me in his field of vision.

Jose took a step in my direction, mere inches from my body. He smelled of cigarettes and cologne, and it stung my nostrils. "Brett's protective of you."

"No, he's protective of his sister."

"Mmm…Yes, Keisha, now there's someone…"

"What do you want, Jose?" I interrupted.

He laughed and leaned down to my ear, hot breath on my skin but not touching me otherwise. "You are very lucky that I'm in a good mood tonight, cochina."

I refrained from rolling my eyes and bit my inner cheek, taking a deep breath to keep from punching him in the face.

He inhaled. "I fucking love the way you smell."

I closed my eyes and inhaled deeply. "Leave me alone."

Jose moaned. "And I so fucking love it when a woman begs. Did you beg Sebastian? I also heard you like it rough." He grabbed the back of my neck and squeezed, bringing tears to my eyes. He slammed his mouth down on mine and forced his tongue between my lips, suffocating me.

I pushed against his chest, but he wouldn't budge, his mouth still invading mine. I heard yelling from behind me as Jose released my lips.

"Oh, yeah, I can fucking see why Sebastian has taken a liking to you, and if you weren't with him, I'd take you so hard right now against one of these vehicles."

"Fuck you, Jose." My lips were swollen and tingling from the rough stubble on his jaw. There was no way I was going to admit to this poor excuse for a man in front of me that I was deeply attracted to his partner.

Jose chuckled and looked down at me. "Oh, cochina, what I wouldn't give to take you up on that offer."

"Stop calling me that," I snapped.

"I'll call you whatever I want to call you," he said.

"What the hell do you want?"

He seemed to think a moment before going on. "You're in love with him, aren't you?"

My eyes widened. "What? No, I'm not." Was I?

"Oh, yes you are." He laughed.

"You're sick in the head."

His brow furrowed and a malicious smile spread on his face. "Oh, cochina, you have no idea."

"Why do you care how I feel about him?"

He shrugged. "I don't. But baby, he's going to eat you up and spit you out. Sebastian Chelios doesn't commit, never has and never will. Especially if I have anything to do with it."

"What the hell does that mean?"

His grin widened. "Oh, you'll see."

"Well, I think you're wrong about him."

"Am I? Give it time. You'll see. He's just using you, and when he gets bored, he'll toss you on your ass."

Anger made my blood boil, and my fists clenched. "Why do you fucking care?"

He rubbed his jaw and thought a moment. "Hmm...I haven't decided yet. I will warn you though, don't try and stay away from him. He will find you. And as long as you play nice, I won't hurt you, even though it is fucking tempting." He leaned down again and ran a tongue up my neck, making my skin crawl. Bile rose in my throat.

"What do you want from me?" I whispered, heart thudding against my chest.

Jose lifted his head and looked down at me, a malicious smirk on his face. He winked at me and turned, walking back the way Sebastian left.

CHAPTER TWELVE

I STOOD THERE, FROZEN in place, and I jumped when warm arms wrapped around me.

"It's just me." Brett's deep soothing voice calmed my nerves, and I took deep breaths, steadying my beating heart.

I swallowed a couple of times before forming the words on my tongue. "I asked him what he wanted from me, and he didn't answer. He just winked at me and walked away. I…he…I don't know what to do. I don't know what he wants."

I sighed, not bothering to tell Brett the whole conversation. That would just make him madder, and he probably already knew what a sadistic fuck Jose was anyway.

"Let's get you home." With his arm still around my shoulders, Brett led me back to his car.

My phone rang as I sat down in the passenger seat, and I saw that it was Keisha. "Hey."

"Oh my gosh, I'm so glad to hear your voice. Brett told me what happened."

"Yeah…" Sliding into the passenger seat, I watched Brett walk around to the driver's side. His stance was gruff, tense…concern clearly etched on his handsome features.

"Are you okay?" Keisha asked, interrupting my thoughts.

"Yeah, I'm fine. Jose is an asshole, and I'm confused all to hell, but I'm okay."

"Well, I'm glad you're okay, but why are you confused?"

"Sebastian told your brother to watch out for me." I didn't understand why Sebastian would say that. Clearly he didn't like him. So many questions pounded in my skull.

"What? He can't stand my brother."

"I know! That's what I don't understand," I said, exasperated.

"Listen, why don't you come over here? We can have a girls' night."

"Can you drive me to your sister's place, please?" I asked Brett.

He nodded.

"We're on our way," I told Keisha and disconnected the call. As we drove to her place in silence, I was left with my thoughts. I didn't know what to do about Sebastian or Jose. I was very confused. Was I falling in love with him like Jose said? I hadn't thought of it until now. I cared for him deeply, yes, but was it love?

I had been thinking that we were getting somewhere, and then all of a sudden Sebastian asked the man he hates to watch over me? Something was going on, and I was determined to find out what one way or another.

Then there was Jose. That man terrified me. Just thinking about him sent ice-cold shivers down my spine. He said he wouldn't hurt me as long as I played nice. What did he mean by that? Was he going to expect me to do something, and if I didn't, then he would hurt me? What had I gotten myself into, and how did I get out of it?

My gut clenched at a thought. Something told me I wouldn't be able to get out of this, and if I did, it wouldn't be easy for me. But the real question was, would Sebastian protect me if I needed him to?

***

We parked a block away from Keisha's and walked the rest of the way. Brett placed an arm around my shoulders, leading me to her apartment building.

I really needed to figure out what was going on with Sebastian. I also needed to talk to him, but that hadn't been easy to do yet. Not knowing how long he'd want me, I considered just playing his game. I never doubted the mutual attraction between us, but now that Jose had said something about him only using me, I wasn't so sure anymore.

Should I continue sleeping with him until he got bored with me? I wanted to. My body buzzed with memories of our one and only encounter. It craved him and the way he made me feel… I wanted that again.

All of these questions flew around in my brain. I didn't even know if Sebastian would want me again, but I knew deep down that he wouldn't hurt me.

"Tori."

"Hmm?" I looked at Brett, and his brows rose with concern.

"Where did you go?"

"I was just thinking." We approached Keisha's apartment, and I walked through the doorway as Brett held it open for me. He followed in behind me and grabbed my hand. I stopped and looked up at him. His smile was sympathetic, reaching his eyes. My heart warmed.

He pulled me into an embrace and lightly squeezed me. "I'm sorry for being an ass earlier, but I'm here if you need anything."

I wrapped my arms around him. He smelled of light, spicy cologne and soap, but it wasn't anything like Sebastian's intoxicating scent of just man and soap.

"Are you guys going to spend all night in the hall?"

My cheeks heated, and I turned to the sound of Keisha's voice. She was standing in the doorway, an amused expression on her face but a hint of suspicion flashing in her eyes. I hoped she didn't think I wanted her brother.

Brett placed his hand on my lower back, and I sighed at his soft touch.

We walked into Keisha's apartment and sat on her couch.

"Tori, did you want to put on something more comfortable?"

I looked down at my tight dress. "Yeah, maybe that's a good idea."

"Come on." she said quietly.

Brett sat on the couch while I went with her to get changed.

She lent me a band T-shirt and sweats. The pants turned into capris since I was taller than her, but they were comfy so they worked. I came out of the bathroom, and she looked me up and down. "It amazes me how you can make sweat pants and a heavy metal band T-shirt look hot."

I shrugged. "Yeah, well, it's all in the boobs."

She laughed. "Probably."

I smiled, feeling somewhat better about tonight's whole ordeal. Before leaving her room, she turned to me, accusation written all over face. "I just have a question for you, and please don't take this the wrong way. What do you want with my brother?"

I had expected this. Knowing I'd slept with Sebastian and then went out with Brett definitely didn't look good from an outsider's perspective. "I just want to be his friend. I'm not interested in him."

She nodded. "I know you two just met, but I can see that he already cares for you. Just…please don't hurt him."

Biting back a scoff, I put on a fake smile. "I don't intend to."

If anyone was going to do the hurting, it would be him. I appreciated her protection over her brother, and I respected her more for that, but if she knew that he was keeping things from her, would she be so willing to protect him? Would I be so willing to protect him if I actually knew what those things were?

A moment later we left her bedroom, and I joined Brett on the couch, curling my feet under me. He placed an arm behind me on the back of the couch. "You okay?"

"Yup."

"Okay, so what the hell happened tonight?" Keisha sat on a lounger that was in the corner across from me.

"I think Tori should be the one to tell you. She was alone with Jose…"

"What? You left her alone with him?" Her eyes widened and her voice rose.

I felt him tense beside me. "I told him it was okay. Jose wanted to talk to me alone, and Brett was nearby."

Keisha turned to me. "Fine, what happened then?"

I took a deep breath. "Jose pretty much guaranteed that Sebastian will not leave me alone until he's done with me."

Keisha frowned. "What's that supposed to mean?"

Damned if I knew. "The way he put it to me, and I really have no idea why he was telling me this, but he said that what Sebastian and I have will be on Sebastian's terms, and it will end when he wants it to end. Jose also said that if he has a say in the matter, Sebastian and I will never be together. Sebastian doesn't commit apparently. Not that I was looking for a relationship or whatever, but still. And apparently, no matter where I go, he'll find me." That last sentence sent shivers down my spine. Was Sebastian a stalker? My libido jumped at that thought.

Keisha rolled her eyes. "So dramatic."

I laughed lightly. "Yeah."

I got up from the couch and started pacing. I had to move, get control of the nerves running through my body.

"Now why does he want Brett to protect you?"

I stopped pacing. "I…I have no idea."

We both turned to Brett. He shrugged. "How the hell am I supposed to know?"

"I think you know more than you let on," I said quietly.

Keisha gaped at us.

Brett's gaze snapped to mine. "What the fuck are you implying?"

I shrugged. I had questions and I needed them answered. "I'm just saying. You seemed pretty chummy with Jose at the coffee shop the other day."

He leaned back in his seat with his ankle on his knee, smirking. "I don't know what you're talking about."

Placing my hands on my hips, I stared back. He was lying, and if I had to call him out on it in front of his sister then I would. "Really?"

Keisha rose from her chair. "Um…I don't know what the hell is going on, but someone better do some explaining right now."

I motioned for him to say something to her, but he didn't. "Did you want to tell her or should I?"

"Tori, shut the hell up," he bit out.

"Hey, that's my friend you're talking to." Keisha glowered at him.

"It's fine, Keisha." I don't know what came over me at that point, but I snapped. "Did you know that Jose and Brett are buddies?"

Her eyes widened.

I laughed once. "Yeah, I didn't think so, and Sebastian wants him to protect me. Please. He must be desperate, and I have a feeling that pretty boy over here knows exactly what is going on."

"Fuck you, Tori." Brett rose from the couch and shoved past me, heading for the door. "You think you don't need protection? Fine. But so help me God, if something happens to my sister, I will make it my dying duty to come after you and your fuck buddy."

I gave him the middle finger as he slammed the door shut behind him. Turning to Keisha, I winced at the shock etched on her face. I sighed, bracing myself for her reaction. "I am so sorry. I don't know what came over me."

She shook her head. "I don't know what's going on with him. He's been so secretive lately."

"I thought I was the only one that noticed." I walked past her and sat on her couch. "I'm sorry. I didn't mean to blow up like that. I usually have more control of my temper."

She sat on the other end facing me. "It's fine. I'll talk to him. He's probably having an off day. I really want you both to get along."

Brett's words bounced around in my head. Maybe he was right. What if my hanging out with Keisha brought harm to her? I could never live with myself if something happened to her because of my poor choices. I rose from the couch. "Maybe I should go."

"No, you don't have to leave."

"What if Brett's right?" Tears welled in my eyes, but I forced them back.

"Nothing is going to happen to me because of you. And besides, it's not your fault that you're irresistible."

I laughed, swiping under my eyes. Plopping back down on the couch, I sighed, loudly. "Ugh…this shit sucks."

"Do you want a drink?"

"Sure, but no tequila." I didn't think I could handle any more tequila at that point.

Keisha laughed and rose from the couch. "Mr. Tequila and I aren't talking anyway, so how about Mr. Beer?"

"Mr. Beer sounds good to me."

She walked back into the living room and handed me an ice-cold bottle.

Popping the lid, I took a long manly-sized swig. My skin sizzled with adrenaline as the anger flew through me over the whole situation. Keisha was a grown woman, but it would be her decision if she didn't want to be friends with me any longer. Brett had no right.

"I don't want you to worry about my brother. He's overprotective, but he means well."

I turned to her as she sat down beside me. "I think Jose wants something from me."

"What?"

I looked away. "I don't know what, and I'm kind of scared to find out."

"You shouldn't go home."

"Where am I going to go?" My gaze flicked up to hers.

"You can stay here."

"Jose doesn't know where I…oh, shit." A thought crossed my mind and I sat up, sitting on the edge of the couch.

"What? What's wrong?"

"I just remembered that Jose called me but he didn't have my phone number. Oh God. What if he can find out where I live? Anyone can find out stuff on the Internet, right? I gave Sebastian my address and phone number. What if Jose got my number from him and now has my address too?" I was rambling, bordering on the point of hysteria.

Keisha rose and placed a hand on my arm. "Hey, Sebastian wouldn't just give out your information."

With a shaky hand, I placed my beer on the table. "What if Jose stole it from him?"

"Tori, you're going to drive yourself insane with all of these what-ifs."

I placed my head in my hands, swallowing past a lump in my throat. "I don't want to see Jose again. I act all cool and ballsy around him, but really he scares the shit out of me."

"He scares me too. Talk to Sebastian. Next time you see him, tell him to stay with you."

"What? You mean ask him to move in with me?" I turned my head toward her.

"Or even just ask him to stay with you for a bit. Talk to him. Tell him what Jose said to you. Maybe he can figure out how to get Jose to leave you alone." She shrugged.

Her suggestions just might actually work. "I can't ask him to move in, but maybe…maybe he would stay with me or something. I'll talk to him. Maybe he can put the fear of God into Jose or something."

She nodded. "Okay, good. Now get some sleep. Maybe that'll help, and tomorrow we can go shopping or something. I have the day off. Oh, and I only have one rule."

I raised an eyebrow. "Oh? And what's that?"

"Whoever wakes up first has to make coffee." She giggled.

I laughed, relaxing somewhat. "Deal."

***

I woke some time later to my cell phone going off. I was still in a daze, but I ended up finding it on the coffee table, forgetting that I put it there when I first got to Keisha's last night.

I noticed the time before I answered it. Some douche was calling me at four a.m. Sighing, I said, "Hello?"

There was no answer. Not asking a second time, I just hung up and placed it back on the table.

Lying back down on the couch, I remembered that Sebastian had wanted me to leave my door unlocked for him. I sighed when I saw a shadow move in front of me.

Bolting upright, I saw a large form move across the room. It headed toward me, and I realized then that it wasn't a shadow.

It was a man.

CHAPTER THIRTEEN

IT WAS A VERY large man. He came closer to me, as if he was a lion hunting for prey.

My heart thudded against my chest and pounded in my ears. I pushed myself back into the arm of the couch as far as I could as a cold sweat broke out on my skin.

I wanted to yell for Keisha, but my throat closed up. I also didn't want him to know that another person was there. I was going to protect her for as long as I could.

As the large man came near me, my eyes squinted and I slowly began to recognize the large form approaching me.

"Sebastian! What the hell are you doing?" I whispered loudly, not wanting to wake up Keisha.

He didn't say anything as he towered over me. His scent oozed off him and dove into my nostrils. The smell of him was overpowering and I loved it. Missed it.

"How did you get in here?" I didn't know how he found me at Keisha's place, and I wasn't sure if I should be freaked out, but at this point, I was so turned on that a part of me found it exhilarating. Like no matter where I was, he could get me if he wanted to, and that set my skin on fire.

Not really giving me a chance to stew over my thoughts, he pulled my legs so I was lying down on the couch with him above me.

"Sebastian. How did you find me?" I whispered. "And why did you break in? You could have knocked."

He chuckled. "That's not how I roll, baby."

"Seriously?"

He smirked and grabbed me by the waist, flipping me onto my stomach. He leaned down, and his hot breath grazed my ear. "I'll always find you, little one."

My skin hummed with excitement at his words. My breathing picked up as his hands ran up under my shirt and caressed my bare back, sending electric shivers down my spine. Now that I understood why he was here, I closed my eyes and sighed, letting him do whatever he wanted.

I knew we needed to talk about what had gone on earlier that evening and about the fact that Jose said he wanted me, but right then, with my sleep-filled brain, I just wanted to enjoy that moment.

His hands smoothed down the sides of my body, igniting my skin under his touch. They skimmed over the sides of my breasts, causing me to squirm at the ticklish feeling.

His fingers reached the waistband of my sweats, and with a yank he had them to my ankles and off of my feet in one quick move.

Cool air roamed over my bare ass, and my heart sped up in anticipation. Liquid seeped between my legs as an aching need throbbed in my loins. I moaned as hands messaged and kneaded my ass cheeks.

"I love your ass, little one," he whispered in my ear.

My breathing picked up, and grabbing onto the couch cushion under me, I fisted the fabric in my hands. My core throbbed. Ached with desire for him.

His hands moved to my knees, spreading them apart so my foot was on the floor, opening me to him.

I jumped and moaned as fingers grazed over my core.

"God, you're fucking wet for me already." He groaned, pushing a finger and then two into me.

"Always." I reveled in the feel of his hands on my body again.

He leaned down, pumping his fingers into my pussy.

Arching my hips, I took his fingers deeper, pushing back against his hand.

He chuckled. "Like that, baby?"

I shuddered as teeth grazed over my tailbone. "Oh yeah."

"Do you like me fucking you with my fingers?"

I moaned at his crude words. "Yes."

"You're gonna break me, aren't you, little one?" he whispered.

I frowned, momentarily confused by his words. Did I hear him right?

His fingers picked up speed, and I quickly shoved what I'd thought I heard to the back of my mind.

I arched my hips as his fingers continued to penetrate me as deeply as they could possibly go. "Do you like that?"

I licked my lips and took a couple of deep breaths. "Oh, yes."

"Good. I want you to come against my hand." His fingers drove in and out of me, igniting a sheen of sweat on my skin.

My breathing picked up as an orgasm slowly brewed.

Fisting my hair, he licked my ear and moved down to my neck. "You're hot for me."

Spreading my legs more, I pushed back against his hand as his fingers roughly penetrated me. "Oh, Sebastian."

"That's it, baby. Come for me. Come against my fingers." He removed his fingers completely and entered me again, filling me, going as deep as my body would allow.

I cried out. A moment later, a tingle spread from inside as he rubbed my G-spot. Shaking, I bit my lip as an orgasm spread from my core.

Sebastian bit my neck gently as he continued to rub that perfect spot deep within me. "Do you want more?" he asked a moment later.

"Yes." I breathed, my muscles still shaking from the orgasm. I heard a zipper being lowered, and my breathing picked up.

Removing his fingers from me, he replaced them with the head of his cock. He ran it slowly over my wet core, teasing me, and I moaned as he finally lowered himself into me, slowly.

The feeling of his clothes against my bare skin as he moved above me made goose pimples rise on my flesh.

His one hand was on my hip, squeezing, holding me in place as he thrust in me. His other hand was on the arm of the couch. He removed himself from me completely and then drove back in slowly, filling me to the brim.

I cried out again and clapped a hand over my mouth.

He chuckled.

I tensed up, waiting for Keisha to catch us, but she never appeared.

Sebastian grabbed my knees and spread them further, giving him better access as he slowly penetrated me.

I felt an orgasm building, but it hovered, not increasing or diminishing. I whimpered and wiggled in frustration.

"What's wrong?" he teased.

I needed him to pick up momentum, and I needed it now. "I need you to go…oh God…"

"What do you want, baby?" He removed his cock from me completely, ran it over my sex, sending shivers through my whole body.

"Please…faster," I demanded.

"Baby, I thought you'd never ask."

I moaned, arching my hips for him.

He chuckled and lifted me onto my knees.

I held onto the arm of the couch and waited for him to give us the release we both needed.

He repositioned himself behind me and paused. "Ready?" he asked, his voice husky.

"Oh God. Yes."

He growled and impaled me so hard that my knees rose from the couch.

I gasped and moaned as he drove into me, surprised at myself that I didn't actually scream. I held onto his wrist, panting at the deep impact. I pushed back, meeting him thrust for thrust as tingles spread through my body.

"You like it deep, baby?"

"Yes," I moaned.

"Good, 'cause I love filling you with my cock."

I panted, loving the way he spoke to me. His erotic words turned me on almost as if they were touching me themselves.

He moved his hips faster, and the sounds of our heavy breathing filled the room. "Oh, fuck."

"Sebastian." He grabbed my ponytail, pulling my head back, and covered my mouth with his. Our tongues meshed and moved as one. Our bodies moved together, and he swallowed my scream as another orgasm shattered my insides, leaving me quaking under him.

"Shiiit." A moment later, he joined me with his own release. Slowing his hips, he kissed me one last time and removed himself from me.

I felt a sense of loss at the emptiness as I flopped back down on the couch, but it was quickly forgotten as sleepiness took over. "Don't leave," I said, yawning.

He kissed me on the nose, that sexy, smug grin of his splaying on his face. "As much I want to bury my cock deep in your pussy again and for the rest of the night, I don't think Keisha would like seeing me here in the morning."

My skin heated at his words, but I was too tired and satiated to argue.

He put my pants back on me and pulled them up to my waist, then covered me with my blanket.

I heard him do up his pants as my eyes grew heavy. I guess my question whether he would be wanting me again or not was answered. Before I dozed off, a warm breath washed over my ear, followed by a light kiss. "Dream of me, little one."

***

I woke up a couple of hours later feeling completely satisfied and happy with myself. Then I remembered why. I hadn't dreamt my late-night encounter with Sebastian, had I? My loins quivered and ached in response. Maybe I did.

Sitting up, I gasped. Areas of my body were sore from all of the attention it didn't usually get. Nope, definitely wasn't a dream.

I did have other dreams of him, though. Naughty R-rated dreams that made my skin tingle just from the memory of them.

Walking into Keisha's kitchen, I found her coffeepot. The coffee was sitting right beside it, so luckily I didn't have to search the whole kitchen for it.

I leaned against the counter, waiting for the coffee to finish brewing, thinking about my visit that morning from Sebastian. My emotions were scattered all over the place as I realized that I probably shouldn't have given in to him so easily. Of course, it wasn't like he gave me a choice, really.

You're gonna break me, aren't you?

Did he really say that, and what did that even mean?

I searched through the cupboards until I found a mug. I brought down two and placed them on the counter. I had just grabbed some milk out of the fridge when I heard a shuffling behind me. I turned to see Keisha strolling in, and I laughed. "Not a morning person, are we?"

She grumbled and made some noises that sounded like a zombie.

I laughed and poured myself some coffee. A thought occurred to me, and I really hated to ask, but I knew I had to. "Keisha…"

She held up a hand as she took her first sip of coffee. I waited as she moaned into her cup.

Turning to me, her eyes were brighter. "What's up?"

Well, that was fast.

Oh, crap, how was I going to ask her this?

I sighed. I was just going to ask and get it over with. "Did you hear any strange noises last night?"

She frowned. "Strange noises? No, not really. I'm a heavy sleeper, and I also sleep with music on, so I don't usually hear anything."

I breathed a sigh of relief and covered it by taking a sip of my coffee.

"Why do you ask?"

"Oh…I just thought I heard something. That's all." I went back to sipping my coffee, my cheeks heating.

"Okay." Her eyebrows lowered as if she was seeing right through my lie.

I turned and walked to the couch. Sitting, I groaned as my sore muscles throbbed.

"What's wrong with you?"

"Oh, my body's stiff apparently. The couch isn't the comfiest. I didn't sleep well." I was such a bad liar.

"Ah." Yup, she could definitely see right through me.

I leaned forward and placed my coffee on the table.

"Why is the door unlocked?"

My eyes widened and I gasped, which then turned into me choking.

"Are you okay?"

I nodded, clearing my throat. Well, that seemed to distract her from the door being unlocked. I grabbed my phone and went to the last message I got from Sebastian. I typed up a quick text reading Next time, make sure you lock the door, ass, and I hit Send.

Maybe then he would think twice about coming to me in the middle of the night and actually call first.

After our coffees and some much needed girl talk, I left and headed for home, needing to get ready for our day of shopping.

As I walked, my muscles tightened and strained against the movement. Memories of my early morning visitor flashed in my head, and warm tingles spread over my skin.

Oh, what I wouldn't give for another visit like that, and soon.

CHAPTER FOURTEEN

A **COUPLE OF WEEKS** had passed since I'd heard from Sebastian or even Jose, for that matter. No phone calls, no late night visitors, Sebastian didn't even show up at the coffee shop. I started to really miss him.

Work was going really well, but the way I was going, it would take forever to pay off my school loans.

Since it was the weekend, I'd decided to stay in and do absolutely nothing, but I was missing something. Since the last time I saw Sebastian, he'd been in every single one of my dreams. Coming to me in the middle of the night, having his way with me, and then leaving right after. I always woke achy and sore for him. Every time I walked past my phone, I picked it up to text him but then quickly decided against it, not wanting to seem in the least bit desperate. But I was desperate for him. I needed him like I needed air to breathe.

Sighing, I grabbed my phone from the table and scrolled to Sebastian's name. I typed up a text. Call me.

My thumb hovered over the Send key. Did it sound desperate? I sighed deeply and hit Send anyway. Would he actually call me or just show up? My loins quivered at that thought. Ah, yes, my body had missed him too, apparently.

Now that I thought about it, he never even responded to my text the morning after the last time I saw him. I frowned at that, and anxiety swirled in my belly. I really hoped everything was okay.

Keeping busy with work had helped distract me from thoughts of Sebastian…somewhat, but not enough. My co-workers were also nice, and my boss treated me well, and it came with benefits.

Keisha and I had regular coffee dates, and I occasionally saw Brett. We would just say hi in passing, but since our fight, I'd decided to stay away from him for a while.

Keisha kept me up to date on the club and how he was doing when I asked, but other than that, she wouldn't mention him.

I knew that I would have to face him sooner rather than later and get this argument settled between us, but right then I wanted nothing to do with him.

I grabbed the channel changer and put down my book, lying back on my couch. My phone rang, and I saw that it was Sebastian calling me. My pussy clenched with desire at just reading his name on my phone. I bit back a groan.

I didn't think he'd actually call me. I really should have learned to never underestimate him. Picking up my phone, I swiped across the screen and placed it to my ear. "Hello?"

"Oh, I have definitely missed the sound of your voice, little one."

"Sebastian." I said. I closed my eyes as the chocolaty smoothness of his deep voice washed over me.

"Mmm…and I've missed the sound of you breathing my name."

My loins ached for him. "It's just you, baby. You're the only man whose name I've breathed."

"Then those men didn't know what they were doing."

I laughed. "No, but you definitely do."

"I do," he said, sounding smug.

"Are you okay, though?" I asked, concern for him filling my voice. I was shocked at how much I was worried for his safety. I was' sure he could take Jose on his own, but that man scared me. He was downright evil.

"What do you mean?"

"I haven't heard from you in weeks," I replied, my cheeks heating at how much I sounded like a nag.

He sighed. "Yeah, business has had some minor fuckups."

I frowned, lying back on the couch. "Okay. I just wanted to make sure you were all right."

"Is that the only reason why you wanted me to call you?"

I chewed on my bottom lip. "Well, no, but that was the main reason."

"What was the other reason, little one?" He said, his voice lowering.

My heart sped up. "I was going to ask you if you wanted to come over."

"I always want to come over, baby."

I smiled. "Good, 'cause my door is always open to you."

"I like the sound of that. Where are you?"

"I'm at home," I answered, turning to the TV.

"Oh? What are you doing?" His voice lowered.

"I was watching TV, but now I'm talking to you."

"Sounds fun."

I rolled my eyes. "Oh yeah, tons."

He chuckled. "What are you watching?"

"Adult cartoons."

"Adult cartoons?" he asked, sounding disappointed.

I laughed. "Were you hoping I'd say porn?"

"Well, yeah."

I smiled, feeling brazen. "Why do I need to watch porn when I have you?"

"Oh, little one, you read my fucking mind. Are you sure you want me to come over?" he teased.

My heart sped up. "Yes, please."

"Would you like that, little one?"

I took a deep breath and sighed. "Oh, yes."

"Good. Unlock your door." And with that, he hung up.

I frowned and threw my phone on the table. I really needed to teach that man some phone etiquette.

Standing from the couch, I walked to my apartment door and unlocked it, smiling to myself when I remembered how he broke it before our first time together.

***

I woke to late night TV awhile later. Gotta love those adult cartoons. Lying on my couch, I realized that I must have fallen asleep.

Rolling onto my back, I frowned. Sebastian had never come over. Disappointment washed over me, and I was surprised at how much I missed him.

My apartment was completely dark except for the glow coming from the TV.

A moment later, the hair on my arms stood on end as I felt eyes wandering over me. My heart sped up as excitement flew through me. "I know you're there, Sebastian."

A deep chuckle came from the kitchen. "Really? Then why don't you come find me."

My stomach flip-flopped and excitement grew inside me. Shivers ran down my spine. I feigned boredom and pretended to yawn. "Please, these cartoons are way more entertaining."

"Is that so?" His voice was deep and sultry.

I giggled and looked toward the kitchen but couldn't see him at all in the darkness. Placing one arm above my head, I sighed. Feeling a moment of bravery, I bent my legs, took a deep breath, and then spread them apart.

I smiled when I heard an intake of breath from somewhere in the dark kitchen. Knowing he could see all of me, I ran a hand up my inner thigh until I reached my core. Pausing, I waited. "You know, it's kind of lonely over here."

There was no response.

"Okay, guess I'm going to have to take care of this myself then." I called out. Placing my other hand on my inner thigh, I brought my finger up to my mouth and inserted it between my lips, slowly sucking on it. Releasing it with a pop, I ran it down my stomach, igniting shivers down my spine. Squeezing my thigh, I smoothed my finger through my wet folds, making myself gasp as I touched the sensitive nub. I bit my bottom lip and closed my eyes as I flicked my clit. Arching my hips, I moaned.

"Make yourself come for me, baby."

My eyes snapped open, and I saw Sebastian standing at the end of the couch. I reached out to him. "Touch me," I begged.

He shook his head, looking down at my hand between my legs. "Come for me."

I groaned and rubbed my clit harder.

"That's it, little one. Make yourself wet for me."

I cried out as tingles spread through my body, and I inserted a finger in my core.

"Are you wet for me?" he said, the words smooth as a purr.

"Yes."

"Use two hands," he demanded.

As I thrust my finger in me, I rubbed my clit with my other hand.

"Are you thinking of me?" His voice lowered as he watched me pleasure myself.

"Always." I panted, imagining it was him pleasuring me. Feeling his rough hands on my body. How could I not be thinking about him when he was right there? A couple of feet away from me. Knowing that he wouldn't touch me yet made the anticipation build up quickly.

"Do you want me to fuck you, little one?"

I squeezed my eyes shut as ecstasy traveled through my body. "Yes, please..."

"Come first. Scream my name, baby," he demanded, his voice firm.

A moment later, I screamed his name as an orgasm erupted from my insides, almost breaking me in two. After the tremors left my body, I lay there panting, watching Sebastian watch me with those beautiful dark eyes of his.

He then walked around to my side and grabbed my hands, but not before I noticed the very large bulge in his pants. It looked like someone else enjoyed that almost as much as I did.

I gasped, my eyes going wide as he took my fingers into his mouth and sucked them. He moaned, his tongue peeking out to lick the juices off of my hand. "Shit, little one."

I smiled. The sound of the TV turning off made me jump. The moonlit glow cascaded around the room but I still couldn't see everything clearly. "Sebastian." I squinted in the darkness. "Seriously?" There was no response. "I'm not a fan of the dark, you know. You never know what's lurking in it."

Still no response. I reached out, feeling for him, but he was no longer beside me. I rose to my feet and was almost instantly attacked from behind, Sebastian pushing me up against the back of the couch.

My breathing was labored as his hands travelled up my body and under the hem of my shirt. "Do you always sleep in just a T-shirt?" Sebastian whispered in my ear.

"Now I do," I moaned. "It's better access."

"For who, little one?"

He knew the answer already. I smiled. "For you, Sebastian."

A deep growl erupted from his throat. "I'd say. I guess I should come over more often then."

My heart jumped at that, and I leaned back against him as he continued running his hands up my body.

"I take it you would like that?" He chuckled.

"Yes…please…"

"I enjoyed watching you touch yourself, little one."

I smiled. "I thought you would."

He sighed. "I've missed you so much, baby." His voice was low, and it no longer carried the playfulness from just a second ago. His calloused hands smoothed down my torso, thumbs grazing my nipples.

I leaned back harder and ground my ass into his hips, feeling him harden against me.

He groaned.

I smiled. I loved having that control, and I loved the way he made me feel…alive. Like a woman who had unleashed her inner animal.

Turning in his arms, I lifted my T-shirt off. My body tingled as I felt him look at me. Kneeling before him, I brought my hand up to his cheek and ran my thumb over his full bottom lip.

He kissed it as it moved. "Little one…" he whispered. His hands moved down my back and cupped my ass, squeezing and pulling me against him.

I linked my hands around his neck and brought his mouth down to mine. The kiss was slow and tender at first, very different from the other times. Something was off with him, but I couldn't quite figure out what it was.

His tongue entered my mouth slowly, as if he were asking for permission. I moaned, but his kiss felt…emotional. He moved from my mouth to my jaw and down my neck, trailing light, hot kisses along the way. Grabbing my breast in a large hand, he kneaded and lowered his mouth to it.

I whimpered out as his tongue circled my nipple, making me arch against him.

Lifting his head, he grabbed my jaw and placed a rough kiss on my lips.

"Sebastian."

He looked down at me and turned me, placing my hands on the back of the couch.

My heart thumped against my chest as I heard a belt buckle loosen and a zipper go down.

I looked behind me and saw Sebastian standing naked behind me, looking at me as if he wanted to devour my very soul. His hooded eyes drank up my naked post orgasmic body, and he took a step toward me. "Hold on, little one."

I turned around and tightened my hold on the back of the couch as he came up behind me.

Wrapping an arm around my middle, he lifted me. Running his hand up my body to my neck, he held my jaw and stuck his finger in my mouth.

I lightly sucked it and gasped as he thrust his cock in me.

He grunted and pounded into me from behind as he held onto my jaw. When he finally released me, he ran his hand through the back of my hair, making goose bumps coat my skin.

"Sebastian."

He groaned, holding onto my hips, and continued to fuck me against the couch.

I cried out as euphoria spread through my body, igniting my blood on fire.

"That's it. Come for me, baby." His hips picked up speed, lengthening my climax. Sebastian's orgasm followed soon after as he shook against me.

Turning me, he wrapped my legs around his waist. I straddled his lap and rested my head against his chest and sighed.

"Did you like that, little one?"

I lifted my head. "I always like it, Sebastian. Actually, I think like isn't even the right word."

He chuckled and then looked serious, as if he was thinking about something.

"What's wrong?" I asked quietly.

He looked down at me but still didn't answer my question.

I frowned. "Sebastian, I think I know you well enough by now to know when something's wrong."

His face was cast in the dim shadow of the moonlight but I could still see him clearly enough to know that something was tugging at his emotions. His hands dug into my ass, and I groaned.

I gasped. "Stop…trying to…distract me."

Instead of answering, his one hand went up to my neck and pulled my mouth down to his.

I tried resisting. I really wanted to know what was wrong, but my body gave into its desires, and I gave up. "Sebastian."

Our mouths moved together as our tongues danced. Panting, I lifted my mouth from his. "I want to feel you."

His breath hitched as I slowly moved between his legs. "Like what you see, little one?" he asked.

Ah, now there was the man I'd grown to like. I wrapped my hand around his cock and smiled to myself when it hardened under me.

"Little one." He placed his head back on the couch and closed his eyes, his chest pumping up and down.

I rose to my knees, still stroking him, and licked his bottom lip.

His tongue peeked out.

I bit his lip before covering his mouth with mine. A deep groan rose from his throat, and I smiled against his lips. Releasing him, I took that as my chance, so I moved off his lap and before he knew what I was doing, I had him in my mouth.

"Oh shiiiiit."

I released him with a pop and brought him back in, taking him to the back of my throat. I could taste myself on him, the acidity warming my tongue. Moving my hand with my mouth, I released him again.

He groaned and I smiled. The way his body responded to my touch made me feel powerful and in control. It was exhilarating, and now I understood why he enjoyed being the dominating one so much.

Licking underneath the veined muscle and all the way to the top and around the head, I closed my mouth over him one more time, relaxed my throat and took him all the way in.

"Little one, God…where did you learn to do that?"

I smiled around his cock and kept stroking him, devouring him with my mouth.

"Shit, Tori, get up here and fuck me now."

Now that's what I wanted to hear. I released him from my mouth, jumped up, straddled him and hovered over his rigid cock.

"What do you want, Sebastian?" I asked, purring. Reaching up, I flicked on the light, needing to see his face.

"Little one, you do not want to fucking play this game with me right now."

"No?" I pouted. "And why not?"

He smirked. "Because I am the creator of this game, and I will own you." He grabbed my hips, lifted me, and dropped me on him, filling me completely and making us groan.

I cried out as he lifted me up and down on his cock. I wrapped my hands around his neck, my fingers running through his hair.

"You like that?"

"Oh…yes…" I cried out as he held my hips, thrusting faster into me.

Bringing one hand up to my neck, he pulled my mouth down on his, tongue diving in between my lips.

"Fuck…little one," he said against my mouth. His other hand went to my ass and squeezed as I continued to ride him.

I cried out when it moved to my clit, and I jumped as he rubbed it.

He rubbed it harder, pressing the swollen nub.

I released his mouth and looked into his dark eyes. We both panted as our bodies moved together.

The desire and affection I saw in his eyes ignited my blood. I realized then that I was falling in love with Sebastian Chelios.

CHAPTER FIFTEEN

LIFTING ME, HE LAID me down on the couch, our bodies still attached, moving and writhing as one. A sheen of sweat coated our skin, making us slick.

Placing a hand under my knee, he pushed it up to my chest as he moved in me. His hips thrust slowly, pulling out almost completely and then driving back in, filling me to the brim. I loved the feel of him inside me, and I couldn't get enough. I was falling in love with him, and I wasn't sure how to deal with that, but at that moment I would just enjoy the way he was making use of my body.

Each time he lowered back into me, an orgasm brewed, rising to the top, waiting to explode from my core. "Oh my…fuck." My eyes rolled back in my head as pleasure coursed through my body.

He chuckled and kissed my knee. "You swear like a dude."

I laughed. "I've had a great…" I gasped as he picked up momentum. "…teacher."

The orgasm erupted from my body, shattering my bones, leaving me quaking under him as I screamed his name.

"Little one, God…" Sebastian shook above me as he released into me. He quivered and twitched.

I was getting comfortable with him. It was familiar. I was starting to know what he liked, what made him tick, and it sent nervous butterflies soaring through me.

He slowed his hips down and covered my mouth with his. Biting and pulling my bottom lip, he sent shivers down my body.

I moaned against his mouth, and he lifted his head, a small smile on his lips.

He let go of my knee, and I wrapped my legs around his waist, keeping us connected. Running a hand down my cheek, he kissed me again. "I could kiss you forever," he whispered.

My stomach flipped, and I ran my hands down his back, grazing over the many scars on his body.

He kissed me again before raising himself off me.

I grabbed my blanket and wrapped it around my naked body, lying back down on my couch.

"Does this pull into…holy shit."

I sat up straight and looked down and saw my cat rubbing his body up against Sebastian's leg. "What? Oh, that's Rooster."

Sebastian looked at me, amusement in his eyes. "He's fucking huge."

I laughed and pointed at my cat. "I think he likes you, which is odd, 'cause he doesn't like anyone except for me."

"Well, I'm glad he likes me. Now, does this pull into a bed?"

I nodded.

Sebastian leaned down and petted Rooster on the head. His muscles moved and stretched, rippling over his bones. He looked up at me, eyes blazing, and he smirked as I watched him.

I cleared my throat. "Yes, this is a couch bed. You just have to…"

He pulled it out from the wall, turning it from a couch to a bed. He flipped the light off, the room getting an eerie glow from the moon. The bed lowered with added weight as he moved under the covers beside me. He didn't ask to spend the night, but he didn't need to. He already knew that I would have said yes. Wrapping an arm around me, he pulled me closer to him.

I closed my eyes as questions clouded my brain.

As he covered one of my breasts with a large hand, I curled into him.

"Sebastian?" I said, opening my eyes.

"Hmm?"

"I'm glad Rooster likes you."

"Even if he didn't, he'd have to get used to me," he said against my neck.

"Oh, and why's that?"

He kissed my head. "'Cause I'm not going anywhere, baby."

I bit my lower lip, heart fluttering in my chest. "I'm glad. So..."

He chuckled. "Do we need to put a label on it?"

I frowned. I wanted to. I wanted to know where this thing with us was going. Maybe it was just sex for him, but for me it was becoming more. "Well, no, but..."

He grabbed my chin and placed a soft kiss on my lips and then my nose. "Little one, there's no one else I want. Not anymore. Does that answer your question?"

My heart swelled. "Yes, but we…we need to talk…about…"

Running a hand over my side, he pulled me back against him, intertwining his legs with mine. "I know, but not right now. I want to enjoy this moment with you, little one."

"Okay, but Jose said…"

"Little one, please do not ruin this moment by mentioning that fucker's name," Sebastian said, his voice turning cold.

"I'm sorry, but there's just something I need to tell you." I tried pleading.

Grabbing my chin again, he turned my head toward his and stared into my eyes intently. I could see the still-lingering emotional turmoil written in his expression, and it broke my heart. A moment later, he placed a soft kiss on my lips, and I turned back around. He pulled me toward him and kissed my shoulder. "Go to sleep, little one."

I sighed and closed my eyes, my I love you going unsaid. I then fell asleep to the rhythmic beat of his heart.

***

I opened my eyes a couple of hours later to the sun shining in my apartment. Warmth spread through me when I realized that Sebastian was still lying beside me. My thoughts went back to last night. My muscles ached from being well used.

I could feel his walls breaking down and that he was slowly letting me in. I didn't know much about the man, but I did know that he was very secretive. We never talked, really. It was mostly physical between us, but I knew that I was falling in love with him in spite of that.

Maybe it was the physical attraction I felt toward him that I was in love with. I wasn't sure, but either way I knew that I felt something strong for him.

Every time we were out, he had to be touching me in some way, especially if we were around Brett or Jose. He seemed territorial...possessive even, but I loved it. Craved it. It let me know that no matter who was around, I was his and only his. Was I really only his, though? He was gorgeous. He could get any woman he wanted, and yet there he was with me.

I didn't expect him to be on the same emotional level as me, but I wanted to pursue this relationship, or whatever it was that we had, further with him. He said he wanted no one else, but what did that mean exactly? I was the only one for him? I guessed that was a start at least. I knew we eventually had to talk about this, but right now, I would savor this moment.

His breathing was deep and even while he continued to sleep.

I ran my fingers over his arm that was under my head. He had a lot of tattoos, but the one that stood out the most was amore written in beautiful cursive on his inner wrist. What made him get love in Italian tattooed on his skin? Was it for a woman? I swallowed past the twinge of jealousy that rose in me and turned onto my back.

I rubbed a hand over the arm that was still around me. His skin was darker than mine, and it made my pale flesh look whiter. I traced some of the intricate designs of his tattoos as I smoothed a hand over his broad shoulder.

Turning back onto my side, I snuggled into him and gasped when I felt his cock press against my ass. My core throbbed, waking up with desire for him. Pushing into him, I moaned as his cock hardened against me.

A deep chuckle vibrated through me, and I stopped, turning my head, my cheeks heating. He was looking at me with intense dark eyes filled with hunger and lust. His lips turned up into a smirk. "Do you like waking up to my cock against your ass?" His deep voice was gravelly, and it made my heart skip a beat.

My mouth parted and my body awoke at his question. "Yes."

"Good." His arm pulled me tight against him, turning me in the process so my back was to his chest. He moved his other arm out from under my neck and swiped the hair off my nape.

I closed my eyes as he placed hot, wet kisses on my neck, sending shivers down my spine. I whimpered when he lightly bit my shoulder. "Like that too, do we?"

I sighed, arching under him. "A little pain never hurt anyone."

He laughed. "That's my girl."

My heart swelled at him calling me his girl.

His other hand roamed down my body, stopping at my nipple. The pad of his thumb brushed over it, sending jolts to my groin. Moving his hand down farther, he lifted my leg, and I gasped when I felt him sink into my slick opening. He grunted. "Always wet for me, little one."

I moaned in response. Now this was the way to wake up in the morning, and it was way better than coffee.

Kissing my neck and moving his lips to my shoulder, he drove in and out of me slowly. It wasn't intense like it usually was, but it was just as passionate. Teeth grazed my skin, sending sharp jolts of electricity through my body. He moved his hips slowly, sending shivers down my body with each thrust.

Tingles spread over my skin as an orgasm exploded from inside me. I cried out as Sebastian sped up his pace, increasing my orgasm. I clenched around him, igniting his own release.

"Fuck," he growled. As he slowed his movements, riding out the waves of his orgasm, a phone rang. Placing one last kiss on my shoulder, he removed himself from me and moved to the end of the bed. Grumbling, he grabbed his jeans.

I sat up and wrapped the blanket around me. Scooting to the edge of the bed, I sat beside him and ran my hands up and down his smooth, hard back.

"This better be a fucking emergency," he snapped. He waited a moment and looked at me, placing his hand on my thigh. "No, I'm not alone."

I placed my leg on his lap and leaned against his arm, wrapping my hands around his big bicep.

He turned back around, listening to whoever had called him. I kind of had a feeling I knew who it was. "That's none of your business," he bit out. "Why should I tell you who I'm with?"

I raised an eyebrow. Okay, obviously whoever was on the phone was starting to piss him off.

"Yes, I'm with a woman."

I frowned, running my hand up to his neck, spreading my fingers through his hair. His eyes closed and his breath caught when I lightly tugged on the soft strands at his nape. He turned to me and raised an eyebrow. I giggled, tugging again.

Keeping his eyes on me, a hint of mischief flashed over his features. He lifted his hand and moved it under the covers.

I gasped when I felt his fingers reach my core and moaned when he stroked my still-sensitive clit. Leaning my head against his shoulder, I cried out as his fingers flicked the hardening nub.

He went back to talking to whoever was on the phone while continuing to bring me over the edge.

I didn't know how he was able to carry on a conversation at that point. Moving my hips against his hand, I shuddered when his finger entered me.

Turning to me, he held the phone away from his ear. Eyes blazing, he said quietly, "Ride my finger, little one. I want to feel you come against my hand again."

Moving to my knees, I did as he demanded.

He replaced his finger with two and thrust in me as I moved against his hand. Letting my head fall back on my neck, I bit my lip as fire exploded from my core. "Sebastian."

He slowed his movements down, and I whimpered. His jaw tightened. "We are partners. You don't fucking tell me what to do… I'll be there when I get there… Who's the one that started this fucking business? Me, and don't you forget it."

He flipped the phone closed and threw it on his pile of clothes. Turning to me, his eyes dark with hunger, he yanked the blanket off me. He rose and pushed me back on the bed.

I arched my hips as his fingers moved faster again. "That's it, baby. Come for me."

I shook and quaked against his hand, crying out his name as another orgasm exploded from inside me.

"Now, I want to taste you."

"Oh, God," I moaned.

He rose above me on all fours and kissed me hard, moving from my mouth to my jaw, down my neck, and between my breasts. As he went lower, I ran my fingers through his hair and pulled when he reached my clit. He lightly ran his tongue over the pulsing nub.

My eyes rolled back in my head and I gasped as a finger entered me. "Oh…Sebastian." I grabbed his hair as his fingers started moving faster, thrusting hard into me. I cried out as my muscles spasmed, another orgasm spreading from inside.

He slowed his fingers down and licked my clit, making me jump, but the build up to my release simmered.

I groaned. Speeding up his fingers again, I cried out as he brought me to the edge and then slowed down again. "Sebastian, please…"

He chuckled against my mound and then lifted his head. My stomach flip-flopped when he licked his lips and moaned. "God, you fucking taste good."

His tongue gave a long lick over my core, and I shuddered under his mouth. "Sweet like honey."

I moaned and bucked under him as his tongue continued to tease me but not give me the release that my body desired. "Please, oh God. I can't take it anymore."

"What do you want, little one?" His voice was hoarse from lust as his gaze bored into mine.

Panting, a sheen of sweat coating my skin, I groaned in frustration. "Please, let me come."

Grinning, he sped up his fingers and covered my clit with his mouth, sucking and pulling me into euphoria. His tongue rubbed hard against my clit as he sucked it in between his lips.

I felt burning from my center as my muscles contracted and started to shake against him, raising my pelvis against his mouth.

Another orgasm exploded from inside, and I screamed, my body shattering from pure ecstasy. His name bounced off the walls as my body shook under him. Before the shocks of my orgasm receded, he had replaced his fingers with his cock, filling me completely.

I cried out as he thrust in me, igniting another orgasm from my core.

He placed a hard kiss on my lips. "God, little one," he groaned, continuing to move in me.

I wrapped my legs around his hips, pulling him into me. I panted, running my hands down his back, scratching him with my nails.

He thrust his cock hard in me, pounding into me with everything in him. His body shuddered against me as he shook through his own orgasm, bringing on another release of my own. Covering my body with his, he rested his head in the crook of my neck and shoulder.

"Sebastian?"

He ran a hand down my arm, taking deep breaths. "I just…I need a second."

I giggled, wrapping my legs tighter around him. He fit perfectly against me, and it was comfortable…familiar. Running a hand down his sweat-slicked back, I smiled as he shivered.

"Little one."

"Hmm?"

"I don't know how to say this." He cleared his throat a couple of times.

My heart sped up. Sebastian was at a loss for words?

"From the first moment I saw you, I wanted you." He rose above me and moved my damp hair off my forehead. His dark eyes swam with heated affection. "I needed to have you. I was drawn to you, baby."

I ran my thumb across his lips. Him admitting his feelings for me, even if it was just the physical attraction he was talking about, raised hope in me that maybe someday he could fall in love with me. "I know that feeling."

He leaned down and kissed me, lightly grazing his fingers down my cheek.

"Sebastian," I whispered.

"I can't get enough of you. You're like a drug, and I think I'm addicted," he admitted.

I smiled, my heart thundering against my chest. "Well, I think I feel the same way."

"Yeah?" A sexy grin spread across his face.

I giggled. "Oh, yeah."

"What are you addicted to most?" His hips moved slowly against me, and I shivered.

"Hmm…" I tapped my chin, pretending to think about it. "I know. Your body."

His eyebrow rose playfully. "Seriously?"

I laughed. "No, of course not. I'm addicted to all of you, baby."

He stopped moving and the playfulness left his eyes. Cupping my face in his palm, he placed a soft kiss on my lips. "Little one, I think I'm…" The phone rang again, and Sebastian tensed. "Shit." He rose from me and reached for his phone but not before placing a kiss on my lips. "What the fuck do you want now?"

I sighed. Would he have told me that he was falling in love with me? No, Sebastian Chelios didn't commit. But maybe Jose was wrong after all.

"Jose."

Lovely.

His shoulders tensed. "Yeah, I'm on my way."

I sat up, leaning on my arms. "What were you going to say before we got rudely interrupted again?"

Sebastian ran a hand over his hair and down his face. Sighing, he turned to me. He rose from the bed and walked over to me. Grabbing my chin, he placed a hard kiss on my lips. "I have to go, but we'll talk later."

I nodded. "Okay."

"We should also do that every time I talk to him. It would make dealing with that asshole a whole hell of a lot easier."

I smiled. "Is there anything else I can do?"

He looked at me while putting on his jeans and thought a moment. Pulling his shirt over his head, he took a step towards me. Leaning down, he cupped my cheek in his hand, thumb rubbing my bottom lip. "Yeah, there is something you can do, actually."

I leaned into his palm and closed my eyes. "Name it," I whispered.

"Stay the fuck away from Jose."

CHAPTER SIXTEEN

A COUPLE OF HOURS after Sebastian left my apartment, I went for a walk. I strode into the coffee shop a little while later. It being the weekend, the place was busier than usual.

I couldn't get Sebastian's warning out of my head, and it set my nerves on edge. Would Jose really hurt me, or was he just being an ass? I didn't trust the guy and clearly neither did Sebastian.

Walking up to the counter, I ordered my latte. "Hey, is Keisha working today?" I asked the barista. I hadn't talked to her in a couple of days, so I didn't know what her weekend schedule was.

"Yup, she's on break. I'll tell her you're here. You're Tori, right?"

I smiled and nodded. After thanking her, I walked to my usual spot by the window and sat down. Looking outside, I got lost in my thoughts. Was Sebastian worried about me? Did he think Jose would hurt me? I wasn't sure, and I really wanted to ask Sebastian, but at the same time I didn't know if I wanted to hear the answer, just in case.

"Hey."

I turned at the sound of Keisha's voice as she sat down across from me. "Hi."

She frowned. "What's wrong?"

"Nothing, why?"

"I know you, and I can tell when something is wrong. You also wear all of your emotions on your face."

Awesome. I took a sip of my latte, and I sighed. "Well, let's see. Where do I begin?"

Keisha leaned back. "Have you seen Sebastian lately?"

"Um…why?" My cheeks heated. Was it obvious that I had seen him? Was there a sign above my head saying that I just had the best sex of my life a couple of hours before with a man who had so many secrets my head spun?

"You have, haven't you?" Her eyes narrowed.

"Yes, I've seen him." I wasn't going to deny it. It wasn't like I was ashamed of it. Whatever happened between Sebastian and I was our business, no one else's.

"Have you been seeing him regularly?"

"Well, whenever I can I guess. Why?"

She sighed, chewing her bottom lip. "We worry about you."

My eyebrow rose. "We or Brett?"

"Well both of us but Brett mostly. He may be an ass, but he doesn't want anything to happen to you."

I laughed once. The way he treated me made it very hard to believe that he actually cared about me. He was jealous, but there was nothing that I could do about that. "Yeah, okay."

She frowned and rolled her eyes.

I appreciated that they worried, but they didn't need to be, not when it came to Sebastian. Now Jose…God, just thinking about him made my stomach clench with uneasiness.

"Tori."

"Hmm? Oh, sorry, what?"

"I asked you if you've seen Jose."

I swallowed. "No, but Sebastian spoke with him this morning." Before she could speculate on the fact that he spent the night with me, I continued. "Jose called him, and I could tell Sebastian wasn't happy. I don't know what he said to him, but Sebastian ended up hanging up on him. He also told me to stay away from him." I thought a moment. "He spoke with someone else too, but I don't know who that person was. He wouldn't tell me."

"Well, at least Sebastian and I agree on something," she mumbled.

"You don't like Sebastian, do you?" I asked quietly.

She sighed. "I never said that. I just don't know if I trust him, but if you like him, I'll try. Brett definitely cannot stand him. I really have no idea what's going on there, though."

"I don't know why either. Something is definitely up with those three, but I still think that Brett knows more than he lets on."

"Tori."

"I'm sorry, but that's how I feel." I knew Sebastian and Jose worked together but where Brett fit in, I wasn't sure. He obviously knew them, but I didn't know how.

"I know, but just drop it, please."

I looked at her and saw the pleading in her eyes. "Okay, I'll drop it."

"I don't know Sebastian personally enough to say that I don't like him, but because Brett doesn't like him, I guess I'm biased. I do see the way your eyes light up whenever his name is mentioned, so I know that you care for him deeply. I just don't trust him."

I leaned my elbow on the table and placed my head in my hand. "I know. I texted Sebastian last night, asking him to call me because I was concerned that something had happened. I was starting to miss him, but I had no idea he would come over." Okay, maybe I did, but I didn't need to confess everything at that moment.

"Did something happen to make him disappear for a couple of weeks?"

"I don't know. I never got a chance to ask." My gaze flicked to hers, and I saw understanding cross her features. She knew why I never had a chance to ask him, but she didn't actually come out and say it. "But he did seem off. I know something happened, I just have no idea what."

"Just please be careful and listen to what he said. Stay away from Jose." Keisha paused a moment and seemed to choose her next words carefully. "Are you falling in love with Sebastian?"

"Uh…well…I…" I stammered. I knew that I was falling in love with him, but I wasn't sure if I was ready to say it aloud yet, especially if I hadn't said it to Sebastian.

She sighed. "For you, I will give him a chance, but if he fucking hurts you in any way, I will castrate him and shove his dick down his throat."

My eyes went wide at that visual. "Okay…thank you?"

Keisha laughed and then turned serious. "Please stay away from Jose."

"Well, I don't plan on searching the guy out or anything, but I'll do my best." A moment later, my phone rang. Picking it up, I saw that it was Brett. "Hey," I answered. "It's your brother," I mouthed to Keisha.

"Hey, yourself." His voice sounded different.

I frowned, looking at Keisha. "What's up?"

"I need you to stop by the club." It sounded more like a demand then a request.

"You don't want anything to do with me for weeks, and now you all of a sudden want me to come to the club?"

Keisha frowned.

"Just get your ass over here, Tori."

"No, I'm having coffee with your sister. I'll get there when I get there." I disconnected the call and threw my phone on the table. Who the hell did he think he was?

"What was that about?"

I looked up at Keisha and shrugged. "Brett wants me to come to the club for some reason."

Her brows rose suspiciously. "Why?"

"I have no idea."

"Did he say what he wanted?"

I shook my head. "No, just for me to come to the club." Which I thought was very odd. Suspicion rang through my body.

"Are you going to go?"

I looked at her and thought a moment, contemplating what I should do. I sighed. "A part of me wants to be a bitch and just not go, but then the curious side of me wants to know what the hell he wants."

Keisha laughed. "Sounds like a struggle."

I smiled, and it instantly fell as my phone rang again.

"Here, let me." She swiped across the screen. "Hello?"

I giggled at her attempt at putting on a sexy voice.

She looked at me, her demeanor becoming serious. "Um...yeah..."

I frowned.

"Yeah, she's sitting right across from me." A moment later she handed me the phone, apology written in her eyes.

I huffed and reached for it. "What?" I snapped.

"Oh, cochina, is that any way to greet a friend?"

My stomach dropped. I needed to get a new cell phone. Jose having my number really creeped the hell out of me, especially when I had no idea how he got the number in the first place. "What the fu..."

Jose chuckled. "Did you ever kiss your mother with that mouth?"

My jaw clenched as anger tore through my bones. "What do you want?"

"Turn around."

Keisha's face paled, and I followed her gaze.

Turning around, my eyes widened at seeing Jose standing at the large bay window.

"Now, stand up and come outside."

"Why?" My heart raced against my chest. There was no way I was going to go outside…

"'Cause I said so."

Shit. "What if…"

"You don't really want me to cause a scene, do you? 'Cause I will." He moved his hand inside his jacket, revealing a gun in the waistband of his jeans.

"Is that a gun?"

I turned to Keisha and looked around the room to see if anyone else noticed the psycho asshole at the window flashing his gun. No one seemed be the wiser as they went about their daily business of drinking coffee and serving customers. Sighing, I rose from the chair.

"Tori, you're not seriously going outside, are you?"

"Give me a minute," I said into the phone and then hung up.

"Tori, you can't do this. Jose is fucking crazy." Her voice rose frantically.

"I have to go. It'll be fine. I promise. I can handle him." I wasn't sure who I was convincing, her or myself, but I wouldn't let Jose win this game he was playing with me.

"Tori."

"It'll be fine. Call your brother and tell him I'm on my way. Please." My heart pounded against my chest as I turned towards the door.

"Okay."

As I neared the door, the grin on Jose's face widened. As he watched me, it made my skin crawl in disgust. What the hell am I doing?

CHAPTER SEVENTEEN

LEAVING THE COFFEE SHOP, I turned left, walking past Jose, and headed in the direction of Brett's club.

Jose came up beside me and placed an arm around my shoulders. Bile rose in my throat as the smell of sweat and cigarettes filled my nostrils. "I'm going to Brett's club."

"I know," he said smugly.

"How did you know that?" Swallowing past the hard lump of fear in my throat, I ignored the way his arm around my shoulders made anxiety swirl in my belly.

An evil grin spread on his face, and he leaned down to my ear. "'Cause I was there when he called you originally."

Crossing my arms over my chest, I sighed. "Of course you were."

"You know me well." A hot kiss was pressed on my cheek, making my stomach clench.

"No, I just know what an asshole you are." I pushed him away and he laughed. I sped up my walk, getting a couple of feet ahead of Jose. I cried out as a tight grip squeezed my neck.

"The next time you walk away from me, cochina, you will fucking regret it." I whimpered as his fingers dug into my neck. "I'm gonna have a talk with my boy.

He's becoming a bit of a pussy. I think he feels something for you."

I dug at his hand on my neck. "I don't know what you're talking about."

He pulled me toward him. "Stop." His fingers squeezed my neck harder, making tears form in my eyes. As we headed to the club, Jose turned to me. "Now are you going to behave?"

I glared at him.

Fury flashed in his black eyes before he pushed me through the open doorway.

I stumbled inside, almost losing my footing. My head was yanked back by my hair, and a hand covered my throat, squeezing. Tears formed in my eyes at the tight hold. I cried out as I was pushed up against the wall. "Jose, please stop."

Bile rose in my throat as Jose leaned his hips into me. "You are so fucking hot," he said, growling in my ear.

"Please. Let go of me." My voice was raspy, and I pried at his fingers wrapped around my throat, relieved when the big hand fell from my neck.

Spinning me around, he held me up against the wall. He grabbed my chin, forcing me to look up at him. He held onto my hip with his other hand, fingers digging into my skin.

Pockmarks and light scars covered his face and neck. He smirked before bringing his mouth down on mine. Bile rose in my throat as his tongue entered my mouth.

I whimpered and pushed at him, but he wouldn't budge. He groaned and deepened the kiss. Trying not to gag, I continued pushing him, but that only seemed to make him hold on tighter. Desperation took over as he continued molesting my mouth. Not knowing what else to do, I reached down between us. He moaned as I cupped him over his jeans.

Grinding his hips into my hand, I smiled against his mouth and then with everything in me, I squeezed the shit out of him. He cried out, releasing me. I took that as my chance, and bringing my knee up, I hit him square in the balls.

"You fucking bitch!" He doubled over, gasping for air, one hand holding the wall while his other was between his legs.

I panted. "Don't ever fucking touch me again, asshole."

"What the hell's going on here?"

I turned and saw Brett standing a few feet away. I looked back at Jose. "Why don't you ask him?"

Turning around, I shouldered past Brett and walked to his office. Walking through the narrow, dim hallway and entering the vast club during the day was always weird to me. It usually had people milling about, cleaning or getting ready for that evening when the club would reopen.

The bartender, who I now knew as Alex, was nowhere to be found either, and that bothered me. I'd become used to seeing him behind the bar every time I showed up here. It threw me off for a second that he wasn't around.

I walked through the empty club and headed down the hallway to Brett's office. The door was cracked open.

Yelling sounded from behind me, but I didn't turn around.

I pushed open the door and sighed, relieved. Leaning against the wall, I brought shaky hands up to my face. I frowned when I looked down and saw that my fingers were wet. I hadn't even realized that I was crying. No man ever scared me like Jose did. Even when my mother had brought home all of her douche bag boyfriends, none of them compared to Jose Alvarez. He was sick and demented and filled my nightmares.

Wiping my face, I took deep, cleansing breaths while I waited for Brett and Jose to join me in the office. I walked over to the minibar and leaned against the wall.

"She fucking kneed me in the nuts, man."

"Yeah, well, knowing you, you probably deserved it."

"What the hell is that supposed to mean?"

"Jose, you're an asshole. You can't expect her to drop everything for you if you force yourself on her."

"Yeah, I can."

I shivered at that thought, not wanting to know how far Jose would go to get what he wanted.

Brett and Jose entered the office. Once Jose noticed me, he glared in my direction.

I rolled my eyes, biting my inner cheek.

Brett walked over to his desk and leaned against it. "Are you two going to play nice?"

I looked at Jose. "That depends."

"On what?"

"As long as he stays far away from me, I won't be tempted to rip off his dick and shove it down his throat."

Jose sneered. "Oh cochina, I am going to have so much fucking fun with you."

"Stop. You leave her the hell alone," Brett warned him.

Ice-cold shivers traveled down my spine as panic and anxiety took form in my belly. Ignoring him, I turned back to Brett. "What do you want?"

Brett turned to Jose and then back to me. "We figured it was time you knew what your lover boy was up to."

My heart picked up speed. "Okay." I motioned for them to continue.

"First off, Sebastian isn't who you think he is."

I rolled my eyes at Jose's cliché-filled statement.

"She's got some serious attitude," Jose said to Brett. He turned back to me a moment later. "If Sebastian doesn't beat it out of you, I will."

"Fuck you." I took a step forward, clenching my fists.

Jose laughed and Brett smiled. What was with him? I didn't understand this whole thing with Brett and Jose, but I had a feeling that Brett only put up with Jose to get what he wanted, whatever that was.

Leaning against the wall, Jose said, "As you know, Sebastian and I are partners. Well, we have a secret third partner that works with us. Can you guess who?"

I sighed. "Hmm…let me guess, is it Brett?"

"Ding, ding, ding. Wow, you sure are quick."

I rolled my eyes. "What do you want? An award?"

Jose walked toward me. "I want you to fucking stay away from Sebastian."

"And why the hell would I do that?"

"Because you're distracting him from getting his job done properly."

I frowned. "I don't know what sort of business you guys run, and I don't think I want to know, but I thought Sebastian was the boss…"

Jose laughed. "Please, that fucker is anything but the boss. He's the muscle. He makes sure we get paid and on time, if you get my drift."

My stomach dropped. "Okay, well, I don't see how I have anything to do with this."

"You're fucking distracting him! But…" He looked at Brett and then back at me, his black gaze roaming over me, making my skin crawl.

"Jose, maybe we should wait until later. I just got a text from Sebastian," Brett called from his desk.

Worry settled in my belly that these two had something up their sleeves to get Sebastian. I didn't want to be there. I just wanted to be at home, snuggled up against him, protected by him. He told me to stay away from Jose, and then what happened? I practically fell in Jose's lap.

Jose took a step towards me and stopped. "Brett," he called while looking at me.

"Yeah."

"Leave." Ice cold fear ran up my spine at being left alone with Jose again.

"What the hell man? This is my office."

"I said leave. Now!" Jose continued walking toward me, his eyebrows narrowing on me.

Brett grumbled as he left his office, slamming the door behind him.

I backed up until I hit the wall. "Jose, please…"

"I fucking love it when a woman begs."

Oh God.

CHAPTER EIGHTEEN

JOSE SLAPPED BOTH OF his hands on either side of my head and leaned into me.

I turned my head away from him and squeezed my eyes shut. I heard him inhale, and bile rose in my throat. "I fucking love the way you smell."

Grabbing my jaw, he forced me to look at him. Covering my mouth with his, he placed a hard kiss on my lips. I squirmed against him, and he released me. "I should beat you for what you fucking did."

I glared at him. "Try it, asshole. Touch me again and I'll cut your balls off."

He chuckled. "You can't do anything if your hands are tied behind your back or…" He licked up the side of my neck. "…above your head."

Cringing, I pushed him.

He grabbed my arms and spun me around, pushing me up against the wall. Hot breath scorched my skin as he pulled my wrists behind my back. "You would look fucking hot tied to my bed."

My heart thudded against my chest, and cold sweat ran down my spine. "Jose, stop. Please."

Squeezing my jaw in his hand, he dug his fingers into my cheeks. "I have a message for you and one for you to give to Sebastian."

"What?" I bit out.

"You better fucking stay away from each other."

My eyes widened. He couldn't control what Sebastian and I did. "Or else what?"

Holding my wrists in one hand, he leaned an arm against my neck, pushing my face into the wall. I cried out at the pressure. "You don't want to know what would happen if I found out that you were seeing each other."

"You can't stop us from…"

"Try me, cochina." I jumped as he slammed a hand by my head against the wall before leaving the office.

Turning around, I sank to the floor, letting out a breath that I hadn't realized I was holding. A moment later, I felt hands wrap around me. I jumped when I realized it was Brett. "Don't touch me." I scrambled to get out of his reach.

"Hey, hey. Calm down."

"No." I pushed him and he fell on his ass. "No, you called me to come over here when Jose was here. You fucking set me up."

"Tori, no, I didn't."

"Yes you did!" I screamed. My chest rose and fell with my rapid breathing. Questions and confusion coursed through me. Who the hell did Jose think he was, thinking he could control whether Sebastian and I saw each other? There was no way Sebastian would let that happen. No one controlled him, not even me.

"No, I didn't. Yes, I called you to come over when Jose was here, but I didn't set you up, not intentionally anyway. There are things going on that I can't explain. You need to have patience." Brett rose to his feet and rubbed a hand down his face.

"Whatever, asshole."

"Tori, if anyone should be mad, it should be me. Do you remember the shit you said to me last time I saw you?"

I looked away guiltily.

"Tori, listen to me," he pleaded, grabbing my hand.

I huffed. "What?"

"Something big is going to go down. I don't know when. It could be days from now, weeks, even months, but I need you to fucking trust me."

I frowned. Everyone kept asking me to trust them when in turn they didn't trust me enough to tell me what the hell was going on. "That's what Sebastian keeps telling me."

He paused, his gaze searching my face. Several emotions passed over his handsome features, but the one that stuck out the most was guilt. What the hell was going on?

My heart sped up. "What?"

He took a deep breath.

"Are you going to tell me to stay away from Sebastian too?"

Brett frowned. "No."

"Really? Why not?"

"Because I know you won't listen to me."

I smiled tightly. "You got that right."

"Tori." He sighed, running his hands over his head.

"What?"

"You have to be prepared."

Uncertainty swirled in my belly. "Prepared for what?"

Brett sighed deeply. "You have to be prepared for the fact that you might not hear from Sebastian again."

My eyes widened. "What? Why?"

"I'm just warning you" was all he said. He walked back to his desk, his demeanor slouched as if he had given up on getting me to understand what was going on.

"Why would you warn me? What did he say to you?" I followed him and tugged on his arm, trying to get him to look at me.

"I don't talk to him." Shoving out of my grip, he sat in the chair behind his large desk.

"Yeah, right. What the hell is going on, Brett?"

He didn't reply.

"Brett, talk to me. Please," I begged.

"Sebastian is leaving."

My stomach churned at his words. He was leaving me. A hard lump formed in my throat, and I blinked back the unexpected tears that filled my eyes. "Leaving? Leaving the city?"

He nodded.

"Why?"

Brett's jaw clenched, but he didn't respond.

"Tell me, please," I begged him, but he wouldn't budge. Not one word came out of his mouth as he turned to his computer. Tears welled in my eyes, and I headed for the door.

"He's going to leave because he loves you."

****

I left Brett's office and headed to the coffee shop. I needed to let Keisha know that everything was all right…well all right at the moment. My heart felt heavy. Had Sebastian left already? Did he leave without saying good-bye?

He's going to leave because he loves you.

Tears rolled down my cheeks. My heart broke that he was leaving the city…leaving me.

We hadn't been lovers for long, but I felt like my soul was shattering, like I was losing a piece of me. I needed to find Sebastian, and I needed to convince him to stay. I also needed to find out what the hell was going on.

Somehow I ended up in front of the coffee shop. Not remembering how I got there, I pushed the door open.

Keisha was behind the coffee counter serving a customer before turning to me. Her eyes widened, and she ran towards me. "Tori?"

I looked at her, but my brain wasn't focusing on her words.

She led me to the back and brought me to a room that had STAFF ONLY written on the door. Sitting me down on a stool, she turned to me. "Did you talk to Brett?"

I nodded. "Yeah, I did." My voice was weak, and I almost didn't recognize it.

"Tori?"

I looked at her, tears welling in my eyes again.

"Oh, Tori." Her eyes filled with sympathy as she pulled me in for an embrace.

Placing my arms around her, I returned the hug. I heard some cries, but I didn't know who they were coming from, and then a moment later, I realized they were coming from me.

CHAPTER NINETEEN

"SHHH…TELL ME WHAT happened," Keisha said, rubbing a hand gently up and down my arm.

I sniffed and wiped my cheeks. "God, I feel like such a fool."

"You're not a fool." Keisha held my hand and squeezed it tight. "Now, tell me what's going on."

"Sebastian is leaving." Fresh tears welled in my eyes, but I forced them back.

"What do you mean, he's leaving?"

I took a deep breath. "Brett said that he's leaving because…because…he loves me." My voice cracked, and I swallowed past the lump in my throat.

Keisha's eyes went wide. "He loves you?"

"Apparently. I don't know how the hell Brett would know this or why Sebastian couldn't tell me himself." Anger and frustration rose in me that I had to find out how Sebastian felt from someone else.

"Maybe he's scared."

"He's scared?" My voice rose, and I pushed off the stool.

Keisha flinched.

I started pacing back and forth. "I'm sorry. He's not the only one who's scared, though. He randomly forces himself into my life, sleeps with me, makes me fall in love with him, brings this evil sadistic fuck into my world, and then decides to leave?"

"Tori."

I ignored her and continued. "We hardly talk, and I barely know him, but I fell in love with the fucker anyway. At first it was just physical, just sex. The best sex I've ever had in my life. Then the last time he came over, it felt different." I turned to her. "It was like I was able to crack a wall. I saw the affection he felt for me in his eyes. I know he cares for me. Maybe even loves me like Brett said. I never expected to fall in love with him, Keisha, but I fell hard and fast."

Keisha walked up to me. "You can't control love."

My voice broke, and a sob escaped my lips. "He can't leave me. If he leaves, Jose gets his way."

She frowned. "What do you mean, Jose gets his way?"

"Jose told me that Sebastian and I have to stay away from each other. He's ruining business, or I'm a distraction or something. I don't know."

"Tori," she whispered.

"Sebastian can't leave…I…I…I need him. I…love him. But I can't even get a hold of him. What if it's too late and he's left already?"

"He couldn't have left that quickly."

I looked at her and sighed. "Brett also told me that something big is going down."

"Yeah, he told me that too. I really don't know what that means. I feel like he's been watching too many movies." She joked, trying to lighten the mood.

I laughed lightly. "Yeah, that definitely sounds like a line from a movie."

She smiled.

My phone rang, and I practically dove for it, hands shaking. "Hello?"

"Hello, little one."

I breathed a sigh of relief. "Sebastian. Where are you?" I demanded.

"I'm on my way to your place." His voice sounded gruff.

"Okay, I'm headed home now. We need to talk, Sebastian."

He sighed. "Yeah, I know."

The line disconnected, and I stared at my phone for a moment. "This is it. He's leaving me. I can feel it." Fresh tears filled my eyes.

Keisha placed an arm around my shoulders. "You don't know that. Maybe Jose's bluffing."

I took a deep breath. "Yeah, I hope so."

***

The walk to my place seemed to take forever. People milled about and went on with their daily lives, not even knowing that there was a crazed psychopath on the loose.

God, for Jose to pull out a gun like that in the middle of a public place, who knew what else he would do to get what he wanted. I shivered at the thought of him hurting me or worse.

Once reaching my apartment, I unlocked it and headed inside. Throwing my keys on the table and kicking off my shoes, I walked to my bedroom. A moment later, I heard the apartment door shutting.

"I'll be out in a second. There's beer in the fridge…" My voice trailed off as the hair on the back of my neck tingled. I looked up and saw Sebastian slowly walking into my room, his gaze instantly finding mine. It had only been a couple of hours since I'd seen him, but it felt like a lifetime nonetheless.

The air around him crackled and fizzled with tension as he sauntered toward me. My heart sped up in anticipation.

As he approached me, he looked at me through hooded eyes, hunger and desire flowing through them.

I could see light bruising on his face, and his lip was a little swollen, but finding out what happened to cause that could wait. He needed me and I needed him.

"Sebastian." I breathed the name.

He stopped. Inner turmoil danced in his eyes as his gaze bored into mine. "I need you so fucking bad right now…baby…I…"

I closed the space between us, placed my hands on his cheeks, and brought his face down to mine. He tensed under me as I covered his mouth. Licking his full bottom lip, I slowly drove my tongue into his, sucking and pulling as I went. I wanted to bury myself under his skin. Stay in his arms forever. I wanted him fast and hard, leaving us both sweaty and spent from passion.

A deep groan came from the back of his throat as he relaxed under me, returning my kiss. He ran his hands down my back and cupped my ass, pulling me against him.

I moaned when his erection pressed into my lower stomach. I needed to touch him. To feel his hands all over me. Inside me and out.

His hand ran up my back and to my neck, fingers curling in the hair at my nape. Whatever turmoil he felt before quickly disappeared as his tongue moved roughly against mine, devouring my mouth.

Grabbing my ass, he lifted me and pushed me hard onto my dresser, sending items flying and falling everywhere.

I wrapped my arms around his neck, tightening my legs around his hips, digging my heels in his ass.

He ground into me and released my mouth, kissing along my jawline. Moving his hips in circles, he rubbed against me, torturing us both. My pussy throbbed and ached for him as he continued pushing his hips into me.

I panted and fisted his shirt at his back, lifting it over his head. He took a step back to remove it completely and threw it behind him.

I licked my lips at the sight of him.

His piercings sparkled in the sunlight, and his muscles twitched as if he was holding back.

"Take what you need, baby," I whispered and sat up and grabbed the hem of my shirt.

His heated stare followed my movements and he licked his lips. "How bad do you want me?" His shoulders relaxed at my words, and I knew this was going to be intense.

I lifted the shirt over my head and threw it at him. "I need you hard and fast."

"Do you, now?" He smirked. Catching the fabric, he brought it up to his nose and inhaled.

My heart skipped a beat as a low growl came from his throat. "Oh, yeah."

Throwing the shirt behind him, he was on me before I knew what was happening. His one hand wrapped around my neck, holding me in place as his tongue penetrated my mouth.

I moaned against his lips as he deepened the kiss. Forcing me back against the mirror, he reached between us and undid the clasp on my bra, practically ripping it off me. His rough hands kneaded and massaged my full breasts, his fingers pinching my nipples.

I cried out. "More."

He squeezed my nipples harder, sending liquid seeping into my panties. I gasped as the pain and pleasure mixed as one deep inside my core.

Releasing my mouth, he leaned down and took a budding peak between his lips and grazed his teeth over my nipple.

"Oh, God." Shivers ran down my spine, and I curled my fingers at his nape. "Sebastian." Tugging on his hair, I wrapped my arms around his neck and pushed off the dresser, forcing him to catch me before we both fell.

He growled and pushed me back onto it roughly, grinding his hips into mine. Wrapping his hand around my neck, he crashed his mouth to mine, sending tingles through my lips at the rough impact. God, I loved kissing him. He poured his heart and soul into the actions of his body. Instead of speaking with words, he spoke through his touch.

Releasing my mouth from his, I pushed him, holding him back with my foot.

Raising an eyebrow, he watched me take off my bra completely.

I licked my tingling lips and ran my hands down my chest, massaging and kneading my breasts for him.

His eyes followed my movements, nostrils flaring as my thumbs lingered over my nipples.

Reaching my jeans, I had just looked down to undo them when he grabbed my wrists. I pushed his hands away and grabbed his belt. Cupping his erection, I squeezed, probably harder than I should have, but when he bucked against my hand, I did it again.

"Again." He groaned. Looked like I wasn't the only one who liked a little pain with the pleasure. Squeezing him again, I kissed his chest, grazing my tongue lightly over his pierced nipple.

Pushing my hands away, he grabbed the waistband of my jeans and ripped them open, the button popping off.

I held tightly onto the dresser as he lifted me. He pulled the jeans off me one leg at a time. When they were off completely, he grabbed hold of my foot and kissed his way up to my calf as he moved to his knees.

A giggle escaped my lips at the ticklish feeling, and I lightly kicked him, pushing him away.

An evil glint flashed in his eyes, and I gasped when he reached my thigh and lightly nibbled.

I looked down at him as he knelt between my legs. Rising on his knees, he placed his hands on my waist and gripped the side of my panties.

Wrapping my legs around him and keeping my hands at either side of me, I licked and nibbled his bottom lip. His eyes darkened and his lips parted. I smiled when a deep rumble came from his chest.

"Lean back, little one," he whispered against my mouth. "I want to eat your pussy."

My breath caught in my throat at his words, my sex throbbing with anticipation. I looked down at him and he smirked.

Leaning back against the cool mirror, I gasped when my panties were ripped off and cried out when his mouth covered my core. Gripping his hair in my hands, I moaned and writhed under him as his tongue penetrated me. "Sebastian," I cried out harder as my muscles clenched and twitched.

His hands moved to my thighs, holding me in place, spreading me wider for him. He moaned against my mound, sending vibrations through my sex. A moment later he lifted his head and licked his lips. "God, I fucking love the way you taste."

"Don't stop." I breathed, a sheen of sweat coating my skin.

"Oh, baby, I don't plan on it." Two fingers entered me, and I moaned at the fullness of them. His tongue and thumb circled my clit, and his gaze locked with mine.

Panting, I watched him devour me. I bucked under him and tugged his hair, pulling him against me. Gripping the dresser, I slowly moved my hips up and down against his mouth.

His tongue licked up the sides of my labia before closing over the hardened nub. A deep groan sounded from him as he pressed harder against my clit, spreading tingles through my body. "Come for me, baby."

"Sebastian." I shook under him.

"That's it." His fingers thrust in me faster. "Come for me, little one."

I screamed as an orgasm erupted from my core, leaving me quaking under him.

"I love the sounds you make when you come." I whimpered as he gave one last lick. He lifted his head and then kissed my inner thigh. Grabbing me around the waist, he lifted me off the dresser. "Did you like that, little one?"

Shivers ran down my body as his stubble caressed my shoulder. "Yes."

"Do you want more?"

I swallowed. "Please…yes."

He chuckled. "Good." He covered my lips with his, his tongue slipping into my mouth.

Tasting me on him sent my heart aflutter. I heard a belt buckle clinking and then a zipper lowering, making my skin and sex throb with anticipation. I looked down between us and saw his hand wrapped around his cock. My gaze followed, and my skin heated as he stroked himself. Licking my lips, I watched the involuntary bead slip out the top of the head.

"Do you like watching me touch myself, little one?" His large hand moved from the tip slowly down to the base.

My breathing picked up as I stared at him pleasuring himself. I wrapped my arms around his neck and tightened my legs around his hips. "Sebastian."

He set me on my feet and turned me around. "Is there something you want?" he asked, running a hand down my spine, shivers following in its path.

I moaned, arching against his touch.

Lightly swatting my ass, he ran his cock over my core, moving the wetness over me. Spreading my legs, he softly bit my shoulder. Our gazes met in the reflection of my mirror. Seeing him standing behind me, wanting me as bad I wanted him, turned me on to the point of breaking. "What do you want, baby?"

"Fuck me," I demanded.

"Music to my ears." He growled and thrust his cock into me, his gaze not leaving mine.

I cried out as he filled me to the brim and held on to my dresser.

He paused, his hands tightening on my hips as his fingers dug in. "I'm sorry, little one, but I'm going to fuck you hard and fast now."

"Please," I begged.

Grunting, he pulled out of me and thrust back into me hard, lifting me off the floor. His hands squeezed my hips, surely leaving bruises, but I reveled in the fact he lost control with me.

I cried out as he pounded into me, fucking me against my dresser.

Fisting my hair, he turned my head, covering my mouth with his. The passion and the intensity of his thrusts burst into me as his tongue penetrated my lips. His hips moved faster and harder, his fingers digging into my skin. He tightened his hold on my hips as he impaled me, the mirror banging against the wall.

Our mouths continued to move together as he consumed me completely. Left me utterly breathless.

CHAPTER TWENTY

RELEASING MY MOUTH, HE looked down at me, eyes blazing as he continued to thrust in me. Leaning down, he licked up my neck and gently bit my chin.

"Sebastian." I closed my eyes and pushed back against him, meeting him thrust for thrust.

"You are so fucking beautiful."

My breath caught at his words, and I moaned when his lips grazed over my mouth.

His hands moved to my ass and squeezed as he thrust into me. "I can't get enough of you, little one. I can feel you in my bones."

My heart sped up. Watching him take me against my dresser in the reflection of my mirror was intense and powerful. His muscles strained over his bones as he controlled his movements. "I can't get enough of you either," I whispered.

Our gazes locked. "Yeah?"

I smiled and chewed my bottom lip as each thrust ignited shivers through my body. "Yeah."

"And why's that, baby?" He asked, slowing his hips.

"Please…don't stop." I whimpered. "I…I need…"

A mischievous grin took shape on his face as he removed himself from me completely. Turning me, he lifted me in his arms, wrapping my legs around his waist.

I tightened my hold on him as he walked us to the edge of the bed. His features were strong, controlled, and even though he had tested my patience for the last couple of weeks, I realized that I did in fact love him, and it wasn't just a physical connection we had. Most women probably wouldn't have lasted as long as I did, but I was drawn to him. I couldn't get enough of him. He possessed my thoughts, my dreams. Took control of my waking desires.

Sitting on the bed, he slowly lowered me back onto his cock, making shivers run down my spine. "Is there a reason you can't get enough of me?" he teased.

"Yeah. You make me feel good." Riding him slowly, I ran my hands down his chest, lightly grazing my fingers over the multiple tattoos and scars. His muscles twitched and moved slightly under my touch. Rubbing my thumb over his nipple, I smiled when his breath caught. Looked like they were as sensitive as mine were. Licking my lips, I wanted to taste them. To taste the cool metal of the barbell between my lips mixed with the soft skin of the permanently hard nub.

Following my movements, he pinched my nipple with his fingers, making a hiss leave my lips. My pussy clenched at the sharp but pleasurable pain. "I think you would look hot with your nipples pierced."

My eyes widened, liquid heat pooling in my groin at the thought.

He smirked. "Or maybe something else would look just as good."

Images flew through my mind at his suggestion, but I wasn't sure what exactly he meant.

Leaning his head down, he took a hardened nub in between his lips while keeping his gaze on mine. "Something that wouldn't pierce but would be just as hot."

"Like what?" A glint of something flashed through his eyes, but I couldn't make out what it meant. He didn't answer my question, and it left me wanting more. I wanted to know what he wanted to do to me, and him not telling me right away made the anticipation of not knowing all the more hot and wonderful.

"You'll see in time," was all he said.

"Okay." My breathing picked up at the mention of future encounters with him. I smiled. Should I tell him? "Why can't you get enough of me, Sebastian?" I asked instead. I clenched around him and his breath caught.

"Fuck." His fingers dug into my ass, shivers running through his body.

"Why?" I asked again, snickering and moving my hips against him, riding him. I grabbed his chin, following the same move that he always made on me, and covered his mouth with mine. Biting his bottom lip before thrusting my tongue into his mouth, I loved the way he groaned and tightened the hand on the back of my neck, deepening the kiss. I moved against him, bringing us both to ecstasy.

"Faster, baby," he grunted.

I panted, lifting and lowering myself on him as I rode him, giving us both the release that we desired and craved.

"Fuck. Me," he groaned.

I grinned. "Oh, baby, I am. I so am."

"Oh, yes you are, aren't you?" His other hand squeezed my ass, and holding onto my hips, he lowered us both to the floor. His head fell back, resting against the bed.

Running my hands down his sweat-glistened chest, I grazed my teeth over his stubble-shaded jaw and licked down his neck.

My head was yanked back, and Sebastian's tongue entered my mouth.

I jumped when his finger pushed against my clit, and I cried out against his mouth.

"Come again for me, baby." His finger pushed and rubbed harder against the nub.

"Oh, Sebastian." I screamed against his mouth as an intense explosion erupted inside of me.

A moment later, Sebastian moaned, shaking under me as he felt his own release.

Removing my mouth from his, I stopped moving and looked down at him. Running my hand down his cheek, I rested my head against his shoulder. The erratic beating of my heart slowed to a steady rhythm, and I sighed.

"What happened today?" I lifted my head and ran a hand over the dark bruising on his cheek.

He tensed under me. "How do you know something happened?"

"You have bruises, and your eye is puffy." I ran my thumb over his lips. "And your lip is swollen." Leaning down, I placed a soft kiss on his mouth. "And when you got here, you were upset."

"I wasn't upset."

I raised an eyebrow. Clearly it was going to be harder to get answers from him than I thought.

He rolled his eyes and brought his knees up to his chest with me still sitting on his lap. "Fine, yes, I was upset, but I feel better now."

Leaning against his knees, I smiled, knowing that I had helped him feel better. "So what happened?"

He sighed and ran a hand down my back. "Jose and I had a disagreement."

I frowned. More like he had a disagreement with Jose's fist. "What was your disagreement about?"

"It's not important."

"Sebastian. It obviously was important enough for him to punch you in the face."

"I don't want to talk about it."

"Fine." I huffed. "I know something is going on with you two and Brett, but I honestly don't really give a shit about that right now."

His eye brow rose in warning. "Little one."

I continued and braced myself for his reaction. "What I care about is what Jose said to me today."

His gaze flicked to mine, his demeanor tensing. "What did he say to you?"

Swallowing past the dry lump in my throat, I sighed. "He said that if he has it his way, you and I will not be together."

"Fuck."

"Brett also told me that you were leaving the city."

His gaze snapped to mine.

I looked down and ran my hands over his chest. Tracing small circles around his pierced nipple, I took a deep breath and went on. "He said that you were leaving because you love me."

His breath caught, and he grabbed my hand. Bringing it up to his lips, he kissed my knuckles. "Look at me, little one."

My heart beat erratically against my chest at the thought of never seeing Sebastian again. I'd fallen for him hard and fast, probably from the very first moment I laid eyes on him.

"I said look at me." The commanding tone of his voice sent shivers over my skin, and my eyes instinctively responded to his tone. Affection and adoration swam through his gaze as his dark eyes bored into mine.

Moments went by where neither of us said anything to each other. Anxiety swirled around in my belly at being told that he loved me. I didn't know if it was true. Could Sebastian even love? Or was he even a one-woman man?

"Little one. How do you think I feel about you?" His gaze didn't leave mine, and I couldn't look away even if I wanted to. The intense stare froze me in place.

Chewing on my bottom lip, I sighed. "I…I'm not sure."

"You're not sure?" he repeated.

"Well, I know you care about me, and I know you said that there's no one else you want, but…" I looked away that time and moved to get off of him.

"But what?" He grabbed my hips, stopping me.

I sighed. "I don't know, Sebastian. I never thought of it until Brett said something and then Jose asked if I loved…" My breath caught at my outburst, and my cheeks heated.

Pinching my chin, he placed a soft kiss on my mouth. "I don't care about that. I just want to know how you feel about me. Tell me. Do you love me, little one?"

"I…" Words caught on my tongue. I did love him, but could I say it aloud?

He kissed my jaw. "Because…" He then moved to my ear. "…I…"

I moaned as he lightly bit it, making my core throb.

"…think…" He licked down the side of my throat. "…you…" Covering my nipple with his mouth, I gasped as he sucked and pulled at the hardening peak. "…do."

My eyes shot wide as his teeth grazed over the bud. I coughed, clearing my throat. "Now why would you think that?"

A sexy grin took shape on his full lips as his tongue circled around my nipple. "Why?"

I nodded, arching into him.

"Because."

"Because why?" I asked.

Lifting me, he laid me on the bed facedown, spreading me out under him. He kissed my back, trailing a finger down my spine.

I held onto his wrist and whimpered when a finger entered my pussy. Widening my legs, I lifted my hips. Taking the hint, Sebastian lowered into me, filling me completely. I kissed his wrist and lightly bit it, holding onto it as his hips started moving, thrusting his hard cock in me.

I moaned and trembled under him. "Why do you think I...oh..." His hips sped up, going as deep as he could and stopped. I clenched around him, loving the feeling of being filled by him.

"Because—" He leaned down to my ear and grazed his teeth over my shoulder. "I love you, Tori."

My heart skipped a beat and warmed at hearing him express his love for me.

"Now...tell me."

I smiled. "What do you want to know?"

He growled in warning, still not moving his hips. "Little one."

I laughed and arched under him. "Please."

"Say it and I'll give you what you want."

Was I ready to say it? I did love him.

Placing both hands on either side of my head, he kissed my cheek. "Do you love me, Tori?"

Looking into his deep, dark eyes that had entranced me from the very beginning, a part of me was scared to tell him how I had felt, knowing that this man could hurt me. But he loved me. Taking a deep breath, I smiled. "I do. I love you, Sebastian."

"Oh, little one. How did I ever live before meeting you?" Sebastian growled, pulled out of me and slammed his cock back into me.

I cried out at the deep impact and held onto his wrists, bracing myself.

"Tori, you feel...oh God, you feel good." Sebastian impaled me so hard that I could feel him to my womb.

Panting, I lightly nibbled his forearm, grazing my teeth over his skin. "Yes. Oh…my…"

Grabbing my hips, Sebastian pulled me to all fours and ran a hand down my back, not losing the momentum of his deep thrusts. He pushed my upper half down onto the bed and continued pounding into me.

"Sebastian."

He reached a hand around and I jumped when it grazed over my clit. Mixed sensations ran through my body as he continued rubbing the hardening nub. A moment later, he grabbed my hand and brought it to my mound, spreading my fingers through my folds. I bucked as we both rubbed my clit at the same time. "Come for me."

Sebastian kept his hand on mine as I rubbed the swollen nub, sending sparks of intense pleasure coursing through me.

"That's it, baby. Make yourself come for me. Now."

The command in his voice set me off, and I screamed as a fast explosion shattered my body, leaving me breathless.

A deep guttural growl left Sebastian as he released into me a moment later. Both of us satiated and spent, he laid on top of me, kissing my shoulder.

I sighed and pulled his arm tighter around me. As I curled our fingers together, my eyelids grew heavy.

"Sleep, Tori." Sebastian trailed light kisses across my shoulders, relaxing me. "I love you, baby."

A peaceful bliss washed over me as I fell asleep to the whispers of Sebastian's I love you.

***

The sound of a loud pop made me jump. Sebastian lifted from me, and I followed his movements. He turned his head to the wall and tensed beside me. "Shit."

"What the hell was that?" I asked, alarmed.

He slowly turned back to me. His eyes darkened, outrage and hatred soaring through the brown depths.

"Sebastian." Anxiety filled my belly as my heart pounded in my ears.

A phone rang from behind me, and Sebastian looked up. His jaw tensed as he stood and helped me to my feet, where I noticed a quarter-sized hole in the wall just above my bed. "Is that a gunshot?" I spun on Sebastian.

Walking past me, he picked his jeans up off the floor. Reaching into the pocket, he fished out his cell phone and placed it to his ear. Taking a deep breath, he answered. "You got my attention, fucker."

Holding the cell phone between his shoulder and his ear, he put on his jeans.

I went to my dresser and quickly threw on a bra and panty set and pants. Grabbing a tank top out of my drawer, I turned, pulling it on over my head. A moment later, glass shattered, making me scream.

"Shit! I told you I'm fucking listening, asshole," Sebastian yelled.

I turned to Sebastian and cried out. Blood was coming from a wound on his shoulder. "Shit."

Grabbing a shirt from my open drawer, I quickly pressed it to the wound. My heart pounded in my ears as Sebastian continued to swear into the phone. I didn't hear anything he was saying as I continued to focus on stopping the blood. "We have to get you to a hospital," I said quietly.

"What?" Dark eyes bored into me. "No, I wasn't talking to you. God. You think shooting me is going to get me to cooperate?"

"Sebastian."

He continued to look at me as I soaked up the blood with my shirt. "No…" Sebastian laughed, and then his voice lowered, turning deadly. "Fuck you, Jose. Anything happens to her and I'll fucking come after you. You think your daddy beating you was torture? You haven't seen anything yet, cocksucker." Flipping the phone closed, he threw it across my room.

I chewed on my bottom lip as nervous butterflies flew through my body. "What are we going to do?" I asked tentatively.

His eyes darkened. "We aren't doing anything. You are going to go on with your life. I will take care of Jose."

"Sebastian."

"Don't," he snapped. Grabbing the bundle of fabric from my hands, he held it against his shoulder and walked across the room. "Do you have any duct tape and gauze?" he asked me.

I went in search of the tape and found it in a box of things I didn't use or think I needed. Running to the bathroom, I grabbed some toilet paper. "I have no gauze."

He grabbed the items from my hands. "This is fine."

I helped him tape up his shoulder, but I couldn't help but think that he needed more than just some tape and toilet paper.

"This is my problem, little one. I brought you into it and I'm going to fucking fix it."

Yanking his T-shirt off the floor, he quickly pulled it on over his head, leaving his hair messier than usual. God, he was delicious. Clearing my throat from those thoughts, I took a step toward him. "But what if you can't? What if Jose comes after…"

Sebastian spun on me. "Don't even finish that question. You hear me?"

I flinched.

"If that douche bag did anything to hurt you…" Rage and fury flew through his eyes, and his chest rose and fell with ragged breaths.

I quickly walked up to him and placed both my hands on his cheeks, bringing his face down to mine. "Hey, okay. I'm sorry. Nothing will happen. It'll be…"

"I have to go." He shoved out of my grip and headed for the door.

"Sebastian."

His gaze flicked back to mine.

"Are you coming back?"

He paused before reaching the door. Taking a deep breath, he walked back to me. Grabbing my face, he covered my mouth with his.

Placing my hands on his waist, I pulled him towards me. My lips parted, letting him in.

His tongue ran across my bottom lip before entering my mouth.

I moaned as our mouths moved together.

He lifted his lips from mine and stared down at me. My head spun at the passionate kiss, leaving me breathless. "Little one," he said, his voice husky. "I want you to promise me something."

My heart beat a mile a minute against my chest. "What?"

"I want you to promise me that no matter what the fuck happens, you know that I will come back to you."

I frowned. "Sebastian."

"I will come back to you. I don't want you thinking that I left you. I love you. God, I love you. So much, baby."

Tears welled in my eyes at his words. "I love you too."

"I was broken until I met you. You're my glue," he said softly.

A sob escaped my lips, and I fisted his shirt, clinging onto him, never wanting to let him go.

Wrapping a hand around the back of my neck, he pulled me toward him. "I'm out. I'm going to tell Jose that I am done. I can't fucking do this anymore."

My eyes went wide. "But what if Jose freaks out, or what if something happens to you?"

"Nothing is going to happen to me."

"Sebastian, you don't know that." I tried pleading with him. Jose was evil, and I knew he wouldn't take it well being told that Sebastian quit. No one just quit that lifestyle, even I knew that.

"It'll be fine, baby. Please, trust me."

My arms went around his waist, hugging him. Squeezing him. Letting him know that I would always be waiting for him, no matter what happened. Tears burned my eyes, and I let them fall.

Sebastian grabbed my chin and tilted my head up to meet his gaze. Placing a soft kiss on my lips, he wiped the tears from my cheeks. "I am so fucking sorry."

I scowled. "You're sorry? Why?"

Pain and agony flashed through his gaze, and he placed another kiss on my lips. "Promise me," he said against my mouth.

"Sebastian, you're scaring me."

"Promise. Me." His voice seemed desperate, and it set my nerves on edge.

"I promise."

"And when I leave, you have to stay here. You can't follow me, little one."

There was no way I was letting him leave there without me. He needed me. "Sebastian, let me go with you."

"No!" he yelled, punching the wall beside my head, making me jump. "I will deal with Jose. You stay the hell away from him."

Fear curled in my belly, knowing that this was probably the last time that I would see him for who knew how long. My stomach clenched with nausea, bile rising to my throat. I had a feeling that this wouldn't end well. "I'm just trying to help. We…"

"Fuck, little one. Stop. Please. Let me deal with him. I can handle him. You have no idea who you're messing with."

I quickly ran to the door and stood in front of it. "No. What if something happens to you? I just found you. I can't lose you. Please."

"Little one, move."

"No. I'm not letting you leave. Please, Sebastian, I have a bad feeling about this."

"I said fucking move now!"

I flinched but held my ground. "Why are you doing this?"

"I need you to get out of my way before I make you." His eyes darkened, and his brows narrowed to pinpoints.

"No, you can't force…"

Grabbing my arms, he tried pushing me out of the way.

I dug my heels into the ground. "Let go of me."

"Then back the fuck off." His fingers digging into my arms, I winced.

"I'm just worried for you. You need to get your shoulder checked." I swallowed past the lump in my throat.

His eyes softened. "I'm sorry, baby. My shoulder will be fine. It's just a graze. But please…let me go. If you trust me, you'll believe me when I tell you that I will be back no matter what happens."

I took a deep breath and moved away from the door.

Grabbing my chin, he placed a rough kiss on my lips. "Be patient, little one."

He opened the door, and without looking back, he left.

I sank to the floor and brought my knees up to my chest. Placing my head in my arms, I let the sobs take over my body.

CHAPTER TWENTY-ONE

FOR THE NEXT COUPLE of days, I moved around like a zombie. I should have gone after him. I should have forced him to stay or begged and pleaded harder. Would he have listened to me if I had thrown myself at his feet? I couldn't shake the feeling that something had happened or that something was about to happen. My chest ached with loss. I really regretted not fighting harder for him to stay, but with the memory of him telling me not to chase after him banging around in my head, I had stayed back.

I had to actually drag myself out of bed every day. My body was stiff, anxiety making a home in my belly.

God, I missed him. I knew he would get in touch with me if and when he could, but as each day passed without hearing from him, the hope inside me slowly dwindled.

I never thought that loving someone this much could be so painful, and I didn't know when I would see him again or if I would even see him again. The thought of not having his gentle hands on my body, seeing his sexy grin, or hearing his deep gravelly voice broke my heart and shattered my soul.

I couldn't believe that he was gone. All because of Jose. That asshole had caused so much grief in my life in such a short amount of time. I sighed, frustrated and angry at the world.

I scrubbed my face with my hands as tears threatened to resurface and spill down my cheeks. Who knew someone had this many tears?

Keisha called me several times, but I always ignored the phone. I didn't want to talk to anyone. I didn't want to see anyone. I called my work and told them I had food poisoning, so that bought me a couple of days off at least.

I tried calling Sebastian at the number he left for me, but he wouldn't reply to my text messages or even call me, and that ended up making me cry harder. It may have been desperate of me, but I needed to see him or at least speak to him. I just wanted to make sure that he was all right.

About a week into my state of depression, I got a phone call from an unknown number. My heart skipped a beat at the thought that it could be Sebastian. I answered the phone, my heart thumping wildly against my chest. "Sebastian?"

"Sorry, cochina."

Tears formed in my eyes, and I sighed in frustration. "What do you want, Jose? And why the hell did you shoot Sebastian?"

"Well, don't you sound all cheery? Trouble in paradise?" he teased.

"I don't have time for your shit. What do you want?" I asked again.

"Wow. He really fucked you up good, didn't he?"

I frowned. "No, it was all you. You shot him. Are you crazy?"

"Yes but there is a reason for everything."

What the hell are you talking about?"

"I told you that you two wouldn't be together."

"Thank you for that reminder."

He laughed. "So, where the hell is your lover boy anyway?"

"How the hell am I supposed to know? We're not together, remember?" He left me.

"Oh, but I think you know more than you're telling me. Where did he say he was going when he left your place?"

I sat up. "He didn't tell me."

"Don't fucking lie to me because I know he was on his way to me."

"If he was on his way to you, then shouldn't he have been there by now or made an appearance?"

Jose chuckled. "Sebastian likes to lay low for a bit before pouncing. Actually, I can see that he's on his way to me right now."

My eyes widened. "What? How do you know that?"

"GPS, ever heard of it?"

I could picture his slimy grin in my mind, making my skin crawl with anger. I hated this man. For the shit he put Sebastian through. For ruining our lives and trying to control our relationship or lack thereof. I hated him, and I hoped he'd rot in hell.

"I tracked him just like he tracked you."

My stomach dropped. "You're lying."

"Open up the back of your cell phone and then tell me I'm fucking lying."

"Whatever. I don't care." I didn't care. Worry for Sebastian overtook the suspicion I had all along on how he always found me. It should have freaked me out. Maybe I was sick and twisted that it didn't, but at that point, I didn't care. I just wanted him back safely in my arms.

"Oh, I think you do. Sebastian had control of your life since he first saw you at the coffee shop. You misplaced your phone, remember?"

My heart beat against my chest as the memories came rolling into my head.

"Sebastian left to get coffee and came back and you were looking for it. He told you to check your bag again and magically, there it was."

Sebastian had stolen my phone. He put a bug in my cell phone to track me. That's how he was able to find me at Keisha's. How could he expect me to trust him? My heart broke, and I felt like it was being ripped in two. No. That was Jose's goal. I wouldn't let him win. He wanted me to hate Sebastian so that I wouldn't trust him. I wouldn't let that happen. We had our issues, and our relationship was messed up, but Jose could kiss my ass. A lump formed in my throat, and I swallowed past it. "How do you know that?"

"I know all."

"You're a sick bastard. What do you want?"

He chuckled. "Hmm…I don't know. Maybe to gloat."

I hopped off the bed and paced my room. "What are you talking about?"

"I knew it wouldn't work between you two. You're both from very different backgrounds."

I frowned. "How do you know what my background is?"

"I can tell…"

"Listen, I am sick and tired of you thinking you can control…"

"No!" he yelled. "You fucking listen to me, you little bitch." His voice turned deadly. "You fucking hear me?"

Stopping me in my tracks, anxiety swirled around in my stomach, and I took a deep breath, cringing at the threat in his voice. Sebastian, where are you?

"Understand?"

"I'm listening," I whispered.

"Good girl. Now, the reason for my call. Sebastian showed up here today…"

"You just asked me if I knew where he was headed."

"I know what I asked you. I wanted to see if you would tell me, but since you didn't, next time, I'll just have to fucking beat it out of you."

"Fu…

"Watch it, cochina," he warned with a growl. "Now what I need for you to do is get your gorgeous ass over here."

I leaned against my desk. "Excuse me? And why would I do that?"

"Oh, I don't know," he taunted. "Maybe because if you don't, I'll shoot your fucking boyfriend."

My stomached clenched. "You already did, asshole."

He chuckled. "Oh, yeah. I did do that, didn't I? And I'd fucking do it again."

"You wouldn't dare." I swallowed past the bile that burned my throat.

An evil laugh erupted from the phone. "You haven't learned anything, have you? Call my bluff, see if I care, but if I have to come get you myself, let me tell you, little girl, you won't fucking like it."

The line disconnected, and I sat up, heart threatening to burst out of my chest. A moment later I received a text with the address where I was supposed to go. Taking a deep breath, I rose from my spot at the desk. My eyes scanned my room, memories of Sebastian flying into my brain. Bile rose in my throat again at the thought of him being shot again or worse.

I swallowed several times and attempted to breathe past the nausea, but it didn't help. Running for the toilet, I threw open the lid and emptied my stomach contents into the cool basin.

When my belly was finished torturing me, I leaned against the wall. Tears ran down my cheeks, and my throat burned. Standing up, I quickly brushed my teeth, removing the sour taste from my mouth. A moment of nausea hit me again, and I leaned against the counter, breathing deeply through my mouth.

Being able to move past it this time, I went to my closet and threw on a pair of pants, tank top, and sweater.

I headed out into the living room, grabbed my keys, and left my apartment. Locking the door behind me, a wave of hesitation washed over me. Who knew that Jose would be the one to get me to leave my apartment?

***

"Hello?"

"Keisha." I gripped my phone tight.

"Tori? What the hell is going on? I've been trying to get hold of you for days now."

"I know. I'm so sorry." As I explained to Keisha about everything that had happened, I walked to the end of my street and hailed a cab.

The address that I had been given was in a shady part of town. Now that I neared my destination, I started thinking that I was making a huge mistake. What if Jose was lying and Sebastian was fine? But did I really want to call his bluff?

"Where the hell are you now?"

"I'm around. Listen, I just wanted to let you know what was going on. I'll call you when I can."

"What do you mean you're around? I was about to come over to make sure you're okay and to get you out of your apartment, and you're not even home. What the hell is going on?"

I approached the building, anxiety settling in my stomach after each step I took. "Nothing, I had to step out. Listen, Keisha, right now isn't a good time."

I hung up while she was in mid-sentence. I was definitely not going to bring her into this. The sun was setting as I walked into a playground surrounded by three story walk-ups. The evening air was cool as I wrapped my sweater tighter around me.

I reconfirmed the address that Jose gave me and headed in the direction of the apartment building in front of me. The sound of cats fighting in the distance caused cold shivers to shoot down my spine.

Taking a deep breath, I entered the dingy building, the stale scent of cigarettes and alcohol filling my nostrils. I swallowed a couple of times to avoid gagging and shook it off.

Walking up the stairs to my right, the anxiety in my belly grew stronger and stronger. Graffiti lined the walls, and the puke-green wallpaper was peeling in spots.

Low music thumped through the ground and got louder as I reached the third floor. Before entering the hall, I took a couple of deep, cleansing breaths, trying to control my nerves.

I walked down the corridor and found apartment 3B. My heart jumped and pounded in my ears as I lightly knocked on the door. I waited a moment, but no one answered. Well, that was odd.

Grabbing hold of the doorknob, I slowly turned it, opened the door and walked over the threshold. The apartment was dark, so I felt around on the wall for a light switch, eventually finding one. Flipping it on, the sight of the small place made me gasp. There wasn't a lot of furniture, and it looked rougher than even my small apartment.

The paint was thinning on the walls; a torn couch was against one side in what looked like the living room.

A table filled with garbage on top sat in front of the couch. I didn't know what was lining the table, but if I had to take a guess, it wasn't anything legal.

Not hearing any sounds coming from anywhere in the apartment, my heart beat faster. Why would Jose tell me to come here if he or Sebastian weren't even around?

My phone rang, making me jump. I frowned when I saw the unknown number. With shaky hands, I lifted it to my ear. "Hello?"

"Little one."

My stomach flip-flopped at the deep voice on the other end of the phone. "Sebastian? Are you okay? How's your shoulder?"

"Yes, I'm fine, and my shoulder will heal. Where are you?"

"Jose said that he was going to shoot you again and that if I didn't…" My eyes widened. "Oh God. I'm so stupid."

"Hello? Little one?" The phone line filled with static.

"Sebastian?"

"I can't hear you, baby."

"Sebastian!" I yelled, but the line wasn't clear. He couldn't hear me, and my vision blurred with unshed tears.

"Listen to me, you need to stay the fuck away from Jose. He's lost his shit more than I thought. If he calls you, don't listen to anything he says."

My stomach dropped. "What…what did you say?"

"Little one, listen to me." His voice was firm and commanding, but worry coated his voice.

"Sebastian, can you hear me? He already called me."

Oh God. Oh no.

"What?"

"He told me that he needed me to come help you. He said he was going to shoot you if I didn't show up. God, I'm so dumb."

"No, you're not. Shit. Where are you?"

"I'm at Jose's apartment." I leaned against the wall and slid to the floor. This could not be happening.

"That asshole. I'm going to kill him, you hear me? I'm going to kill that motherfu…shit."

"Sebastian?" My anxiety level skyrocketed through the roof. I heard some shuffling over the phone. "Sebastian?"

"Fuck you, asshole. You've lost your…"

"Sebastian? What's going on?" My heart pounded against my chest as a cold sweat broke out on my skin.

"Jose, you piece of…"

The phone sounded like it was dropped and hit the ground. A moment later, a bang vibrated through my bones making my ears ring. It sounded like someone lit off a firecracker or a car back firing. It was loud, and I couldn't stop replaying it over and over in my head. I realized then that the noise I heard wasn't a firecracker or a car backfiring.

It was the sound of a gun going off.

CHAPTER TWENTY-TWO

"Sebastian? Oh God, please. Sebastian!" I screamed into the phone.

A moment later, I heard the phone being moved and heavy breathing coming through the line. "Sebastian?" Hope filled me, and my heart thumped against my chest.

Then a maniacal laugh filled my ears. "Nope, not your lover boy."

Tears welled in my eyes, and my chest constricted. "What did you do?"

"Something I should have done a long time ago."

"Why? Please tell me you didn't shoot him," I begged. I knew something was going to happen. Sebastian underestimated the sick, evil mind of Jose.

"You see, he was just getting in the way."

My stomach churned, and bile rose to my throat. "How…why…"

"How? Well you see there's this thing called a gun…"

A sob escaped my lips, and I gripped the phone tight.

"And why? Like I said, he was getting in the fucking way. Now that he's out of the picture, you and I can live happily ever after."

This guy was deranged. "What the hell are you talking about?"

"I want you, Tori."

Ice-cold shivers ran up my spine. "Why? Why do you want me?"

"I'm not quite sure, but don't worry, Sebastian isn't dead… yet."

I let out a breath of relief. "Oh, thank God."

"Don't thank him yet. There's still time for that to change."

"Please, what do you want?" My voice was gravelly and came out weak as I tried getting answers. I didn't know what Jose wanted or why he was doing the things he did.

"I already told you."

I frowned in confusion. "I don't understand."

"I want you."

My stomach dropped. "Why? What do you want with me?"

"Well, that I haven't quite decided yet. You see, I'm a fly-by-the-seat-of-your-pants kind of guy, but I think you'd be great leverage."

"Leverage for what?"

"I want Sebastian dead."

A sob escaped my lips.

"Then I can have you, and we can spend the rest of our lives together. I did warn you to stay away from each other."

"We haven't seen each other." I begged him to forgive me. If he did in fact shoot Sebastian again, depending on where he shot him, who knew how long he had to live. I needed to get to him and get help.

"Don't fucking lie to me!"

"I'm not lying!" I yelled. "I gave Sebastian your message and that's it. I haven't seen him at all since you gave me your…warning."

"I know you're lying to me. I know the damage that was done to your bedroom the last time you saw

Sebastian. I shot him, remember? It was me he was talking to on the phone, so don't fucking tell me that you haven't seen him. Or are you that fucking stupid to think you can pull a fast one on me, cochina?"

My stomach dropped. I had forgotten. Not that Sebastian was shot but…it just seemed so long ago since I had seen him that I never even thought of mentioning it to Jose. My days were getting mixed up, but I just prayed that my mistake wouldn't cost Sebastian his life. "What…"

"When you first told him you loved him."

Tears spilled down my cheeks, and my beating heart threatened to burst out of my chest.

"When he told you he loved you back."

He heard everything. "You sick…"

"When he said that he was done. He was quitting the business and coming after me right after I shot him. I was impressed at myself that I had such good aim."

Oh God. "He left after, and I haven't seen him since."

"Oh, I know, sweetheart. Now ask me."

I opened and closed my mouth, not sure what he wanted me to ask him. "I don't know what you mean."

"I know what you want to ask, so just ask already."

I thought a moment. "Do you have my apartment bugged?" I asked weakly.

He chuckled with satisfaction. "Next time, you'll lock your window."

Falling to my knees, I clutched my stomach and dry heaved. Laughter came through the phone, and I threw it against the wall. I continued puking bile as the invasion ripped my privacy away from me. Holding onto my stomach, I gripped it as sharp pains tore through my abdomen. Taking deep breaths, I heard yelling coming from the cell phone. I reached out for it and placed it to my ear.

"Aww, what's wrong sweetheart? Don't like the idea of me being in your apartment while you sleep?"

I cringed. "Fuck you, Jose."

"Music to my ears. Isn't that what Sebastian said before he fucked you?"

"Oh God." My stomach threatened to turn over again. Taking deep breaths, I forced the empty pit of my belly to calm down. "Please, just leave us alone."

He laughed. "Now why would I do that? But because I am a nice guy, I'll give you a head start."

"What do you mean?"

"I mean, you better get running. And I'd lose the cell phone if I were you if you don't want me to catch you quickly."

"Are you seriously…"

"Yes, I'm serious." He laughed again, and then his voice lowered. "Run. Now."

I stared at the phone as he hung up.

Oh dear God, what have I gotten myself into?

***

I headed home but ended up at Brett's club instead, not really knowing how I got there. Walking in a trance-like state, I shook myself out of it once I reached his office door. I had to be strong for Sebastian. Jose could be bluffing, and he might not have actually shot him, but I wasn't going to take that chance.

Before I even knocked on the door, it swung open, and I was pulled into a warm embrace. Brett released me and held me at arm's length, hands on my shoulders. "Keisha called me, freaking out. What the hell happened?"

"I…I…he shot him. Oh God, he shot Sebastian." Sobs wracked my shoulders again, and I fell against Brett.

"What do you mean he shot him? Who shot Sebastian?"

Did he even have to ask? "Jose. Jose shot Sebastian. He shot him in my apartment." I whispered. I wiped at my cheeks and took some deep breaths.

"Shit, Tori." He pulled me in for another hug.

I wrapped my arms around him and squeezed him back. Pulling out of his embrace, I walked into his office. "I didn't want to go home, so I came here."

"That's fine. My door is always open to you."

"Listen, Brett." I took a deep breath. "Sebastian left my apartment and then Jose called me and threatened to shoot him again. And…and…" A sob escaped my lips. "He bugged my apartment." I was rambling, but I needed to get it all out. "Jose told me that if I didn't go to his place, he'd shoot Sebastian, so I went and no one was there."

Brett's face took on a look of shock. "You went to Jose's place? Tori, are you fucking crazy?"

"I didn't want to call his bluff," I yelled. "He said Sebastian was there, and for me to go or else he'd shoot him again. I heard the gun go off. He did shoot him."

Brett sighed. "Okay. I'm sorry. Continue."

"Jose. He broke into my apartment." I shivered and swallowed past the nausea rolling around in my belly.

"Tori…." Concern coated Brett's voice.

The nausea threatened to bubble over.

"Tori, take deep breaths. Breathe. Come on, baby girl, breathe for me."

I took deep breaths, but that didn't work. Pushing past Brett, I ran to the bathroom, spilling my stomach contents into the toilet. The sounds of my dry heaving banged around the small bathroom walls. Leaning my head against the cool touch of the basin, I took deep breaths.

"Are you okay?"

A washcloth was placed in front of me. Wiping my mouth, I sat back, leaning against the wall and gripping my stomach.

"Here."

I opened my eyes and saw Brett holding a bottle of ginger ale. I smiled slightly and took it from him. "Thank you."

"Feel better?" he asked after I took a small sip.

I nodded and then groaned as a sharp pain tore through my stomach.

"Here." A package of saltine crackers was shoved in my face, and my stomach rumbled. I'm sure puking up bile for the last couple of hours didn't do well for an empty belly.

After eating a couple of crackers, my stomach started to feel better and not like someone had hold of it in a vice-grip anymore.

"Now, tell me everything."

I told him everything Jose said during our conversation over the phone. I also told him the message that Jose gave me for Sebastian. "I don't know what to do. I don't know where Sebastian is, so I can't go to him. I don't know if he's okay, and I don't know how to help him. He left me." I sobbed. "I'm so sick of fucking crying."

Brett chuckled, and I turned to him, glaring. "I love your colorful choice of words."

I smiled and let out a tiny laugh through my tears. Brett helped me to my feet, and wiping my eyes, I walked to the couch in his office and sat down. "Yeah, well, it's how I feel right about now."

He sat down beside me, and I leaned my head against his shoulder. "Now, what do you mean Sebastian left you?"

Tears welled in my eyes again. "He…" I swallowed past the lump in my throat. "You were right, but not that he was leaving me because he loves me. I think he's going after Jose. Jose set me up. Told me to come to his apartment or else he'd shoot Sebastian again. I went, Brett. God, I'm so fucking stupid. Sebastian called me. He said he needed to take care of some stuff before he would even consider being with me. Jose shot him. While I was on the phone with him. Oh, God." Sobs wracked my shoulders.

"Hey, you don't know if he did or not."

"But…" He had a point. Jose could have just made me think he shot him.

Brett took a deep breath. "He's doing it to protect you. Maybe you should go stay with Keisha for a while," Brett said softly.

"I can't." Tears welled in my eyes again as I remembered the last time I spent the night at her place.

"Why not?"

"Because Jose knows where she lives." I sniffed and angrily wiped the tears from under my eyes and my cheeks.

Brett tensed. "What?"

"Sebastian knows where she lives, so I assume Jose does too and…." I said quickly.

"What?" He motioned for me to continue.

I huffed. "Jose said that Sebastian bugged my phone."

"Tori, you sure got yourself a winner."

I rolled my eyes. "I know."

"But how the hell does Sebastian know where my sister lives?" I lifted my head, and his dark blue eyes, full of suspicion, glared at me.

"I…Sebastian showed up when I spent the night there," I answered quietly.

Brett's brows furrowed. "Does Keisha know this?"

I looked down. "No, not that I know of."

"How does she not know?"

I turned away and rose to my feet. "She's not dumb, but she hasn't said anything to me about it if that's what you're wondering, and it doesn't matter anyway."

"The hell it doesn't. Are you telling me that Sebastian came to you while you slept at my sister's place?"

I nodded.

"Where was Keisha?"

"She was sleeping." I chewed my bottom lip, waiting for him to respond. Memories crashed back into my skull at the way Sebastian just showed up in the middle of the night, had his way with me, and left. It was wonderful, erotic, and passionate, knowing that he couldn't stay away from me. Maybe under normal circumstances I would have felt used, but this wasn't normal. Our relationship wasn't normal. I took him any way I could, and I reveled in it.

"She was sleeping," he repeated, interrupting my thoughts. His eyes widened as what really happened dawned on him. "So you're saying that Sebastian showed up in the middle of the night to fuck you?"

I cringed at his crass words, and my face heated. I didn't answer. I didn't need to.

"What were you thinking?" His voice rose as he stood up from the couch.

"We didn't disturb Keisha. It's not that big of a deal."

"Not that big of a deal?" He laughed. "God, are you that fucking dumb?"

I glared at him, as anger soared through me at the insult. "Excuse me?"

"I can't believe…no wait, I actually can."

"What the hell are you talking about? Never mind, don't answer that. I'm leaving." I grabbed my bag from the couch and turned to storm out the door but paused before reaching it. "You know, Brett. You, of all people have no right to judge. I know something is going on between you, Sebastian, and Jose or else you wouldn't have set me up like that the other day. So don't sit there all high and mighty like you're the cat's fucking meow, because you're not."

I turned to head out the door when Brett grabbed my arm. "Tori."

"Let go of me." Tears burned in my eyes as he released me. I heard him call my name, but I ran as fast as I could out of the club. He had no right to say those things to me. No right at all. Yes, I had made some stupid choices, but who was he to judge?

I ran all the way back to my apartment. It was only a couple of blocks, but by the time I reached my door, my lungs were burning and the cramp in my side felt like I was being stabbed repeatedly. My fingers fumbled for the keys, and my eyes blurred. Finally finding them, I unlocked the door with shaky hands. Opening it, I took a step forward when I felt arms wrap around me.

I screamed as a hand slapped over my mouth and nose. Kicking out, I hit the door, pushing me back into my attacker.

He grunted and held onto me tighter. I pushed us both back into the wall, making him release his hold on me. I fell to my knees and crawled away from him. White spots danced in my vision, and my breath left me as a big body landed on top of me. "I knew you'd fucking make me work for it."

I groaned as a sweet, sickly scent filled my nostrils, making my eyelids heavy.

"But I didn't realize how fucking hard it would get me."

I tried pushing him off me, but the scent invading my nostrils overpowered my body. "That's right, breathe it in," a deep voice crooned, whispering in my ear as he leaned his hard body into me. My eyes fluttered closed, and I opened them, trying to fight it, but I couldn't.

My eyes closed again, and this time I let them.

"I told you I would find you, cochina." Hot breath scorched my ear as sleep overtook me, drowning me in darkness.

CHAPTER TWENTY-THREE

MY EYES FLUTTERED OPEN, and I tried to lift my head, causing a sharp pain to shoot through my skull. Groaning, I squeezed my eyelids shut, flopping back down on the bed.

Lying on my stomach, I took a couple of deep breaths and tried moving my hands. Needing to rub the pain between my eyes, I realized quickly that I was restrained to the bed. Opening my eyes, I looked at my wrists and gasped. Duct tape was tightly wrapped around them, linking them to the bedposts. I looked behind me at my ankles and saw duct tape wrapped around them also, spreading me out like a star on the dingy mattress.

Oh God, what the hell is going on?

My memory was fuzzy as I tried to recall the last thing that had happened. I looked around the room. The lighting was dim, but it looked like I was in a very small bedroom, the only objects in it being the bed and me.

Then I remembered the fight I had with Brett and the horrible things he had said to me. I also remembered running home and reaching my apartment. I frowned. I never made it inside, and then I ended up here.

Was I drugged? I don't remember what happened in between. No, my attacker had a cloth in his hand. I remembered that, and he held it against my face. I had seen enough movies and shows to know that it was chloroform that I'd breathed in. No wonder I had a killer of a headache. How long I had been there? Who kidnapped me?

I told you I would find you, cochina.

My heart sped up. Oh shit, oh God. Jose.

Panic settled in my stomach, and my breathing quickened. I struggled against my restraints but stopped when I heard sounds outside the room. Male voices carried, but I couldn't make out what they were saying.

I heard footsteps approach the door. The doorknob turned, and I slammed my head back down on the bed, feigning sleep.

"She's probably awake by now."

"What if she's not?"

"Jose said to leave her be and that he would check on her when he gets back."

"Yeah, but I want to see what he finds so fascinating about her."

"No. Stay the fuck out of there. Jose will be pissed…"

"Well, he's not here now, is he?"

"You shouldn't go in there."

Oh, please don't come in here.

The door squeaked as it opened. "I just want to play with her for a bit. What's wrong with that?"

"Jose will chop off your balls and shove them down your throat if you do anything to her."

"It's not like he's going to be gentle with her anyway."

"Yeah, but she's his to do with what he wants."

"Come on, man, what he doesn't know won't hurt him."

"Dude, seriously. Let's go before he shows up."

"What the hell does he want with her then?"

"How the hell am I supposed to know? I didn't ask. Now let's go before he finds us in here."

"Too late, fuckers."

I never thought I'd say this, but I breathed a sigh of relief at hearing the sound of Jose's voice.

"Now get the fuck out of here."

I heard some scuffling and mumbling.

"Leave, before I change my mind."

"I don't know why he gets to have all the fun," one of the guys mumbled.

"Because I'm the boss, that's why." I jumped at Jose's raised voice. "I pay you for your muscle, that's all. Now fucking leave!"

The door slammed shut, and for a moment I thought I was alone. A flicker of hope soared in my chest.

"Fuck," Jose whispered.

Yeah, so much for that idea. I squeezed my eyes shut tighter as I heard him approach the bed. The mattress dropped with added weight as he sat beside me, and a hand brushed my hair away from my nape.

Hot breath scorched my neck, making my skin crawl. His hand roamed down my arm and back up. My stomach churned as hot, wet kisses were placed on my bare skin.

I was still wearing my tank top and pants from earlier, but I felt more exposed now, as if I was completely naked. The kisses stopped, but his hand continued to caress me, sliding down my side. His hand ran under my shirt and smoothed over my lower back.

He moved his hand from my back and ran it down over my ass. I jumped and cried out as he slapped it, sending a sharp pain throughout my body. "I knew you were awake."

I opened my eyes and tears welled in them. "Please," I whispered.

"Please what?" he taunted.

I swallowed. "Let me go."

"Not gonna happen." His hand grazed between my legs, and I whimpered.

Tears leaked from my eyes, and my heart pounded in my chest. "Why are you doing this?"

"I already told you."

I took deep breaths as his hand continued to caress my body.

"I want you," he whispered in my ear.

"Why?"

"Hmm…maybe because Sebastian wanted you or because you're fucking hot and feisty. I haven't really decided yet. Do I really need a reason to want you, though? So stop asking me questions."

Turning my head to him, I frowned in confusion. "I don't understand."

"You don't have to understand. There's nothing to understand."

I tried to ignore the hand moving from my ass to my inner thigh. His touch was rough and painful, and I bit my lip through the pain.

"You're not like most women I've been with. You actually fight back, and it turns me on." He said it so casually, as if it all made perfect sense now.

Oh God. Maybe if I kept him talking, it would delay what I was pretty sure he'd come in here for. "What, are you jealous of Sebastian or something?"

"No!" I felt a sharp pinch on my thigh, bringing tears to my eyes.

I cried out in pain and pulled on my restraints, the tape digging into my wrists and ankles. The pain receded, and I took deep breaths.

"I'm the one who told him about you. I'm the one who showed you to him. And then he goes and fucks it all up by fucking you."

I didn't respond. I had no idea what he was talking about. Sebastian was right, he'd lost his mind.

He stood up and paced the small room. "If he would have just stayed away, I could have had you to myself."

Not on your life, buddy. I watched him walk across the room.

"But no, he swoops in and fucks you before I even had a chance." His chest was heaving as he ran a hand over his shaggy hair.

"Did you really shoot him again?" Tears welled in my eyes, but I swallowed them back, not wanting to give Jose the satisfaction of knowing he was causing me more pain.

My heart ached more at the thought that I would never see Sebastian again, but as long as he wasn't hurt, I could deal with it.

He turned to me. "Wouldn't you like to know?"

"Please, just let me know if he's okay and I'll…" I gulped. "I'll do anything you ask."

His eyes roamed down my body. Walking up to me, he grabbed my ponytail and pulled, tilting my head.

My neck strained against the rough angle, and my breaths came out in short gasps. Jose covered my mouth with his, forcing his tongue between my lips. The stubble on his jaw scratched and scraped at my skin as he invaded my mouth.

He groaned before releasing me. Looking down at me, he licked his lips. "You want to know if he's okay or not? All right, I'll tell you."

My heart thudded against my chest as he leaned his head down and licked a path up my ear. "I killed him. Sebastian is dead."

CHAPTER TWENTY-FOUR

My eyes widened, fury flowing through my body. "You're lying!" I screamed.

Dead? Really? He can't be dead. Oh God. No, please.

"Am I?"

"You can't be serious. How could you?" The tears poured down my cheeks, and I couldn't control them. The emptiness I felt in my chest was almost unbearable. The thought of never seeing him again or touching him, hearing his deep melodic voice wash over me or feeling his gentle caresses because he was dead tore at my soul.

At least if he had still been alive, I'd have a chance. I could give him time and then hopefully he would come back to me. I sobbed harder and started to hiccup. To never see him again… Oh God.

"How? How?" Jose screamed. "I fucking did it for you! So then you and I can be together. He was just in the way."

What he was saying didn't make sense. "Why? Why do you want me? What did I ever do to you?" I sobbed harder.

"Why? Why?"

I couldn't comprehend what was going on right then, so I lay my head back down and let the sadness flow through me.

"You fucking look at me when I'm talking to you, bitch!"

The breath was knocked out of me as I felt him jump on the bed, straddling me. He yanked my ponytail back and wrapped his other hand around my neck. A cry escaped my lips at the rough force.

"You like that, don't you?" Jose moaned in my ear.

"No." I swallowed but couldn't get any more words out with the tight grip he had on my neck.

"Don't fucking lie to me!" he screamed, tightening his hold. "I know you like it rough. I heard the sounds you made when Sebastian fucked you. When he had his cock deep in your tight cunt. You're a whore, and I know you enjoy being fucked like one."

I whimpered. My lungs tightened and constricted at the lack of air. "Please, you're choking me."

He ground his hips into me, and I felt an erection move against my lower half. Pulling at my restraints, I tried shoving him off me.

"I think you fucking like it." His hand moved from my hair down to my waist and ran up under my shirt. Pushing his way higher, he forced his way under my bra, releasing my breast.

"God, you have fucking perfect tits." He cupped my breast in his rough hand, massaging, pulling, and squeezing. He moved his hips against me, grinding into me as he pinched my nipple.

I cried out as sharp pain exploded through me.

"I knew you liked it rough."

My neck hurt from being tilted back for so long, and my lungs continued to burn.

He stopped moving against me and removed his hands from me completely.

Laying my head on the mattress, I gasped when my pants were pulled down to my knees.

"Oh, fuck. Now that's an ass I could dive deep into."

I whimpered and struggled against my restraints as the cool air washed over my naked bottom half. "Please. Don't…oh God."

Rough, calloused hands painfully messaged my ass cheeks, and then they stopped. "What the hell?"

I frowned in confusion.

"Why the hell are there bruises on you? I'm the only one who should leave bruises on you," he yelled. Jose rose on all fours and wrapped my hair around his hand, pulling my head back.

The back of my neck throbbed from the rough impact. "Please…"

"Did Sebastian finally beat you like I told him to? Or did he fuck you so hard he marked your skin?" He ground the words into my ear.

Squeezing my eyes shut, I took a deep breath. I'd seen the bruises after Sebastian left me. They concerned me at first, making me think that I was a freak for liking it rough. No man had ever tested my limits the way he did or made me lose all control, and I knew that he felt the exact same way with me. "I don't know what you're talking about."

"You're a liar."

I gasped as his fingers roamed over my core before entering me. The pain of them violating my unprepared body sent tears rolling down my cheeks.

"Fuck, you're dry and tight. Perfect for my cock. Good thing I like it raw." He continued to thrust his fingers in me and licked up the side of my neck.

I let out a breath I hadn't realized I was holding when his fingers left me. Looking behind me, I saw him rise, grabbing something out of his pocket.

He tapped a cigarette package against his other hand before pulling out a smoke. He pulled out a lighter and flicked it, moving it in front of my eyes, teasing me. Bringing it back to him, he lit the cigarette that was between his lips. He inhaled, and the glow from the ember lit his face. Taking the white stick from between his lips, he exhaled slowly and leaned down, blowing smoke into my face.

Coughing, my eyes burned as the strong, putrid fumes filled my nostrils.

He laughed and sat back up.

I jumped at the sound of a knock coming from the door.

"What the fuck do you want?" he yelled.

"We have a situation," a male voice said from the other side of the door.

"Give me a minute."

"Boss, Sebastian is on his way over."

My eyes widened. Sebastian wasn't dead.

Jose growled. "Shit. Leave. Now. Don't let him fucking near here."

My throat burned from the coughing, but I started laughing. My laugh turned hysterical, tears rolling down my cheeks.

He tensed above me. "What the hell?"

"I knew you were bluffing."

"Oh?"

Through my laughter, I heard the sound of Jose flicking the lighter. My moment of happiness was short-lived when white-hot pain exploded from my inner thigh.

"Here's something to remember me by, bitch."

I screamed and tugged at my restraints as the blinding pain tore through my bones, the scorching-hot lighter marking my skin.

An evil chuckle bounced around the room as he got off me. Grabbing my chin again, he kissed me in between my cries.

I cringed as he licked the tears off my cheeks.

"You're beautiful when you cry. Next time, we won't be interrupted. I'm gonna fuck you so hard you'll pass out from the pain."

I whimpered.

He chuckled. "You're going to love it, my little puta."

I jumped as he ran a finger over the burn, sending fresh pain through me. "Now you'll never forget me. Every time you see the scar, you'll remember me." His voice lowered. "I'll be with you forever." He let go of my chin, and I rested my head against the mattress.

A moment later, I cried out when a sharp pain erupted from my ass cheek. He bit me.

"God, I love your ass." He pulled up my pants. "And I can't wait to drive my cock into it."

"Fuck you," I said weakly.

"Oh, I plan on it, cochina." He smacked my ass before heading to the door.

Bile rose in my throat at his words.

"Don't wait up." He laughed again as he left the room.

My head fell forward on the bed as I breathed through the burning pain coming from my thigh. He had burned me. I couldn't believe he burnt me.

The pain lowered to a dull ache as I continued to think about what Jose had in store for me. How was I going to get myself out of this?

Oh, Sebastian, please come for me. Save me from this nightmare.

I heard noises coming from outside the room that sounded like yelling and then a door slamming shut. Sighing, I closed my eyes.

A moment later, my eyes startled open when something wet touched my hand. Turning my head, I stared into big brown eyes on a head larger than my own.

"Why, hello there," I whispered. A large dog whimpered and whined, nudging at my hand.

"Aren't you handsome?" I tried looking at the collar around the dog's neck to find a name and saw that it said, Malvado.

I didn't know much Spanish, but I did know that that word meant evil. "You're not evil really, are you puppy?"

The dog started panting and licked my hand again, making me smile. A part of me thought maybe the dog was abused because I couldn't imagine Jose loving anything except for himself, but the dog seemed happy so maybe he did.

Tears welled in my eyes. "Oh, Malvado. How am I going to get out of this mess?"

The dog nudged my hand. Sighing, I looked at my restraints.

Did Jose and the guys leave? Oh God, I hope that one guy didn't come back, the one who wanted to play with me. Not wanting to find out, I set to work on getting out of my restraints. I would not give up. If it meant me getting hurt—or worse—in the end, at least I went down fighting. I had to be strong. I wasn't sure how long Jose had kept me locked up, but hopefully it wasn't long enough that people had started wondering where I was.

Brett and I may have had our differences, but I knew he would be worried, and I didn't want that. I know Sebastian wouldn't want me to give up, so I started pulling on the duct tape.

Starting with my right hand, I pulled and bit back the pain of the tape squeezing and scratching my wrist. My arm muscles burned and tightened against the excessive use as I continued pulling.

The bed started squeaking because of my movements, but at this point I didn't care if anyone heard me. I was not letting Jose touch me again. Hope rose in my chest as my wrist made it halfway through the tape and then after what felt like forever, it slipped out.

Taking a deep breath, I waited a moment, and ran a hand down Malvado's head. The dog licked my wrist and trotted out the door.

Happy tears ran down my cheeks as I clenched and unclenched my hand. It hurt but nothing too bad. I was more exhausted than anything. I looked at my other wrist and then back at my ankles, this was going to take a while. With my free hand, I started ripping and pulling at the tape on my left wrist. It was easier to get my other wrist out, but when I looked at my ankles, I really had no idea how this was going to work.

I rose on all fours and fixed my clothes so that I was covered, cringing at the painful memories of Jose touching me. My pants rubbed against the burn on my inner thigh, and it stung.

Taking a deep breath, I stretched my legs so one was straight, pulling at the tape and bent my other leg so I could reach my ankle.

A bang came from outside, and I paused, heart beating against my rib cage. A cold sweat broke out on my skin at the possibility of getting caught trying to break free. Someone yelled, cursed, and with another bang, I was left alone in silence again. I breathed a sigh of relief and went back to working on the tape at my ankles. It started to tear, and I quickly got it off me. Then I went to my other ankle, and as adrenaline pumped through my veins, the process of removing the tape happened much quicker.

Hopping off the bed, I stood and then fell to the floor as my wobbly legs gave out. I rose to all fours and crawled to the door, ignoring the pain on my inner thigh. I placed a hand on the doorknob, lifting myself off of the floor. I strained to hear any noises, but it sounded like no one was around. I peeked my head out the door and looked into a dim hall. There was a closed door across from me and then another closed door to my right at the end of the hall.

I opened the door completely and stood on shaky legs. Walking out into the hall, I followed it to a living room that looked vaguely familiar. I looked around but didn't see my sweater or my bag anywhere, so I headed to the entrance.

I looked back at the place I had been held captive in for who knows how long, and then my eyes widened. This was the apartment Jose had told me to come to earlier. It still had the same dingy smell from before and had the same trash littering the tabletop.

Before I left the room, I saw a cell phone sitting on the table. Not wanting to spend any more time here than I had to, I quickly grabbed it and walked back to the door. Opening it, I braced myself for an attack. I frowned when no one caught me. An unsettling feeling rose in my stomach as I left the apartment. This was too easy.

Where were the guys from before? Where was Jose? He wouldn't leave me here by myself, would he? Maybe he'd underestimated me and thought I wouldn't have the balls to get myself out. I wasn't sure, but I sure as hell wasn't sticking around to find out.

As I headed down the hall, I flipped the phone open and dialed 911. The dispatcher picked up instantly, and I told her that I was being held captive, but I didn't know where I was, not being able to remember the address. "Please, help me," I cried.

"Ma'am, who am I speaking to?"

"Tori McLeod."

"How old are you, Tori?"

"Twenty-four." I quickly ran down the hallway. As I was barefoot, the carpet was rough on the soles of my feet, and my body ached from being in the same position for so long.

"Who's holding you against your will?"

"His name is Jose Alvarez."

"How do you know him?"

"Um…he's my boyfriend's boss." I didn't know what to call our relationship, so I said the first thing that came to my head. I rubbed my arms when a cool draft enveloped me and shivered when a cold sweat broke out on my skin.

"Describe your surroundings."

I told her that I was in a three-story walk-up and in an unsafe part of town. My heart pounded against my chest, making my ears ring as I headed down the stairs. When I got to the main floor, tears of happiness and excitement clouded my vision. When I approached the exit, I stopped. "He's here."

"Ma'am? Who's there?"

"Jose. He's back." Jose was standing behind the door with his hand paused at the lock. My eyes widened. "I have to go now."

"Don't hang up the phone. Stay with me."

"I need to go."

"Ma'am!"

I turned and ran down the main hallway.

"Fuck."

I heard him yell as I made my way through to the other side. I didn't turn back to see if he was chasing me, but I had a good guess that he was. I left the apartment building and ended up in front of a parking lot. It was getting dark out, so it would be easier for me to hide. I praised God for that.

Running into the parking lot, I looked left and right but saw no signs of Jose. He must not have followed me down the hall because he wasn't behind me either. The parking lot didn't have very many vehicles, but it had enough that I could hide behind if I needed to. I ran towards a van when a bang erupted beside me and a car window exploded. I screamed and turned around. Jose was walking towards me with a gun in his hand and a malicious smile on his face.

CHAPTER TWENTY-FIVE

I FELT DIZZY AND light-headed as he approached me. The gun wasn't aimed at me, but he was holding it, stalking me, his black eyes following my every move. "I wouldn't run if I were you." His voice came out deep, almost like a growl.

"Ma'am."

Turning, I ran behind a van just as another window exploded, this time from the van I was leaning against. "He has a gun," I told the dispatcher and then hung up, hoping they'd still be able to find me.

He was shooting at the windows. Oh God. He could hit me.

The parking lot was in between apartments. I saw another lot full of cars and a street. Gunshots in this neighborhood wouldn't strike up much attention, but with me calling the police, I prayed they would get here soon. I just hoped they could find me.

My heart pounded, and my lungs were on fire. My feet were sore from the rough gravel biting into my skin. I took a deep breath and pushed off the van I was leaning against and ran.

Running in front of the vehicles, I headed for the other apartment building.

More explosions sounded behind me. He was taunting me. Not wanting to shoot me intentionally. He was playing with me.

I forced my legs faster. Just as I was about to reach the safety of the big brick building in front of me, my hair was pulled from behind me. I stumbled as the cell phone flew out of my hand. Having been yanked from behind, I fell backwards onto my ass. Sharp pain shot up my tailbone, and I grabbed the hands pulling at my hair. I screamed as I was dragged from behind, and I clawed at the hands ripping at my hair.

"Ow, fuck." The hands loosened their hold, and I pushed forward, rising to my feet when they got pulled out from under me.

I kicked and screamed at my attacker, struggling under the weight above me. My arms gave out as I tried pushing him off me, but my muscles had no fight left in them.

Jose loosened his hold on me and spun me onto my back. His black eyes looked down at me, but I didn't see the gun anywhere. He grabbed my chin, and I tried moving my head out of his strong grip. "You will regret escaping, cochina." He wrapped his hand around my neck and tilted my head back. He leaned down, and I slapped him. The sound echoed in the air as his dark eyes went glacial, but a smile formed on his face. He leaned down again, and I slapped him a second time. "You can hit me all you want, but it won't fucking do anything. I like it rough, remember?"

I went to slap him a third time, but he caught my wrist, forcing it above my head. I moved my legs and wiggled under him, trying to get out of his strong hold.

"You keep moving like that, I'm going to fuck you into the ground."

I stopped, my chest rising and falling, my breath coming in short gasps. This was it. I was going to die. There was no way I could get out of this.

"That's my girl. We don't want our first time to be in public now, do we?" His hand caressed my cheek and moved between my breasts.

I closed my eyes as I swallowed past the lump in my throat.

"Open your eyes."

I shook my head. I couldn't look at him. I didn't want to see the way he looked at me. The lust in his eyes that I had seen before sent ripples of fear through me.

His grip on my neck tightened. "I said, open your fucking eyes. I want you to look at me when I touch you."

The rough grip on my neck left me no choice but to open my eyes. My breathing was labored as I gasped for air.

His hand moved to my stomach, and his fingers grazed the waistband of my pants. He paused as ringing came from the phone a couple feet away from us.

I struggled against him, twisting my body as I tried to reach for the phone.

He slapped me, momentarily dazing me as spots shot in front of my eyes and a bitter taste formed in my mouth when I licked my lip.

Pushing at him with everything in me, I hesitated as something black and metallic danced in front of my vision.

Jose moved it down to my stomach and ran it up under my shirt, the cold metal smoothing over my skin.

I shivered, my heart pounded in my ears, and a sob escaped my lips. "Please stop," I begged.

He moaned. "God, I love it when you beg." He ran the gun up and down my stomach.

Curling his hand in mine, he lowered the weapon into the waistband of my pants. "Move and I'll shoot you."

I closed my eyes, tiny sobs escaping my lips. "Please, stop. I'll do anything you want me to, just please don't shoot me."

He licked up the side of my neck. "Anything?"

I swallowed, taking deep breaths. "Yes, anything," I whispered.

"Oh, cochina, we are going to have so much fucking fun togeth— What the fuck is that?"

I opened my eyes as he turned his head. I frowned in confusion as he got off me, and then I heard it too. Sirens sounded in the distance, and hope flared in my chest. He looked down at me, rage darkening his features. "Did you call the fucking police?"

"No," I lied. The sirens came and went, leaving us in silence. I moved to stand, but he kicked me in the stomach, almost making me throw up instantly.

He kicked me again, and I fell back on the ground, gasping for air.

"No," I wheezed. "I didn't call anyone."

"Liar!" he screamed and kicked me again.

I coughed and rolled over, grabbing my stomach.

"I won't let them take you. You're mine. You hear me? You're fucking mine!"

I rolled to my side just as he kicked me again, and I fell back, pain exploding from my middle. My lungs were on fire as I breathed through the pain.

Jose paced in front of me, his eyes moving about, and I heard the sirens getting closer to us. A maniacal expression filled his face when he stopped. Looking down at me, he pointed the gun in my direction. "If I can't have you, no one can."

My eyes went wide as I stared at the barrel of the gun. A moment later, his cell phone went off, and without taking his eyes off of me; he reached into his pocket, bringing the phone to his ear. "Yeah…oh, hello, Sebastian."

I let out a breath as tears welled in my eyes. I heard yelling coming from the other end of the phone as I moved to get up.

"Tsk, tsk. You won't get anywhere with language like that." He turned in the direction of the sirens, and I took this as my chance to escape.

Rolling over and biting back the pain, I crawled to the phone a couple of feet away from me and tried to get to my feet, crying out when a foot pushed me into the ground.

"You can't have her, asshole. She's fucking mine now, and there's nothing you can do about it." He taunted.

"You wanna fucking bet, asshole?"

My heart skipped a beat at the deep voice coming from in front of me.

"Fuck you." Jose dug his foot harder into my back.

"Sebastian." I cried out at the pain spreading through my body.

"Let her go, Jose."

Jose laughed. "You see, I can't do that. I know my little puta wants me. Her body throbbed for me earlier. Her hot cunt was nice and tight for me too."

Sebastian growled at Jose's words. "Let her go. This is between you and me, Jose, not her. Tori has nothing to do with this."

"She has everything to do with this!" Jose screamed. "If I can't have her, no one can and that especially includes you, asshole. You fucking hear me?"

I looked up as a weight was lifted off me. Rising to all fours, I turned and saw Sebastian and Jose struggling.

Red- and blue-flashing lights surround the parking lots, and ignoring the pain in my stomach from where he kicked me, I stumbled to my feet. I took a step towards the parking lot just as two shots rang out. A moment later, white-hot pain exploded from my body. I fell, landing on my knees, and gripped my side.

My vision faded in and out as I saw Jose running in the opposite direction of the police cars. My head spun, and I fought for breath. Tears welled in my eyes as I gasped for air.

Feeling something thick and sticky between my fingers, I brought my hand up in front of my eyes. A deep red liquid coated my palm. Groaning, bile rose in my throat.

Swallowing back the sour taste, I pushed forward on all fours when a strangled noise came from behind me. Turning, I saw a large heap lying on the ground. Tears welled in my eyes as I quickly crawled to the big body.

Biting back the pain, I squeezed my eyes shut when my hand reached cool leather. White spots danced in my vision as I landed on my stomach, no longer having energy to move.

I gripped the leather as a hand grabbed me. Opening my eyes, I stared into the deep brown eyes of the man I loved. "Sebastian."

My breathing was erratic, and my throat felt like sandpaper.

"Little one." Blood leaked from the side of his mouth, and I quickly wiped it away.

Oh God, he's dying. Sebastian is dying. "Sebastian." I leaned my head against his chest and sobs took over my body.

"Little one." He coughed. "It'll be okay."

I looked at him. "Don't leave me. You promised. Don't fucking leave me," I begged.

"I…I'm so sorry, for everything." He coughed again, causing more blood to leak from his lips.

"I don't care about that. Whatever happened…whatever you did, it's in the past. I forgive you. It's done. Just please…please don't leave me." The sobs racked at my bones.

"I love you," he whispered.

I cried harder, tears rolling down my cheeks. "I love you. Please, don't leave me," I begged. "You promised. You can't die on me. I need you. Please."

His hand reached up and stroked my cheek.

I leaned down and kissed his full lips. "Please…God. Stay with me, baby."

"I'm so sorry, little one. Please forgive me." His eyes closed, and he let out a deep breath.

"Sebastian?"

He didn't respond.

"Sebastian!" I checked his pulse. I couldn't tell if he had one or if my mind was playing tricks on me, but a faint beat moved under my fingers so I had hope that he was still alive. "Wake up!" I started punching his chest. "Sebastian, do not fucking leave me. Please."

He didn't open his eyes.

Screams tore through me. He couldn't be dead. Oh God, no.

"I think they've been shot," I heard someone say from above me.

"Sebastian, I love you. You hear me?" I screamed. "I fucking love you. Don't you dare leave me!" Hands gripped my shoulders as one last scream left my body. A moment later, darkness took over, leaving me in a sea of black.

CHAPTER TWENTY-SIX

I STIRRED AS THE sounds of beeping from the machines that surrounded me.

My body felt numb, as if I was lying on a cloud. I heard voices around me, but I couldn't make out what they were saying. Were they talking to me?

I tried opening my eyes, but they felt heavy, and I had no energy to fight it.

"Is…Tori…coming…around…"

Words floated around me as the voices continued talking about me. I didn't know what was going on or where I was. I tried again to open my eyes, but I couldn't.

My limbs also ignored me when I attempt to move.

"…move…"

Move? I'm trying, but it's not working.

Exhaustion took over and I fell back into a dreamless sleep.

***

"Tori?"

I groaned and gasped when a sharp pain stabbed me in the side. What happened to me?

"Shh…don't move."

I opened my eyes slowly, blinded by the light. I squinted and the room darkened. Breathing a sigh of relief, I lifted my arm to rub my eyes but it felt like it weighed a ton. "What…what's…"

"Shhh…you need to take it easy. Lie still."

"What…" I swallowed. My throat felt like a desert, and I licked my lips. Opening my eyes completely, I saw Brett and Keisha standing beside me. "Hi."

They both smiled, and Keisha wiped under her eyes. "Hi," they said in unison.

I frowned, looking down at my body, and realized that I was in a bed. "Where am I?" My voice came out gravelly.

"You're at the hospital," Brett said, holding a glass of water to my lips.

I sucked on the straw, letting the cool liquid coat my throat. "What happened?"

Brett and Keisha looked at each other. "Maybe you should get some more rest before we go into that."

"No…please…" Images flashed into my mind. "Oh God, I remember." I was shot. Jose shot me and beat me and…and touched me. "Jose…" My breathing quickened, and something started beeping faster.

"Hey, calm down. He's not here." Brett grabbed hold of my hand. "He won't hurt you again, and Tori…"

I looked around the room and took deep breaths, trying to calm my frantically beating heart.

"Tori." I looked back up at Brett. "God, I am so sorry."

He was sorry? "For what?"

"I'm sorry for the horrible things I said to you. I'm such an asshole. Will you ever…" he knelt beside my bed, squeezing my hand. "Please forgive me."

Unshed tears blurred my vision, and a lump formed in my throat. I nodded. "Of course." My voice was hoarse as I remembered how things had been left with him.

He sighed in relief and stood up, placing a kiss on my forehead.

A nurse in peach-colored scrubs came into my room. "Oh, I see you're awake." She had a friendly smile with warm blue eyes, and even though she seemed nice enough, it didn't help the horrible feeling that continued flowing through me. Besides me being in the hospital, something was off, but I couldn't figure out what.

Checking my blood pressure, she frowned. Turning to Brett and Keisha, she said, "I don't want you upsetting her."

"They didn't upset me," I responded for them. My voice still felt raw, and the nurse pushed over my tray, handing me the glass of water. I took another sip, letting the cool water soak my aching throat.

Once the nurse was satisfied, she turned around, and before heading out of the room, she said, "Ten minutes and then Tori needs to rest."

When the nurse left, I turned back to my friends.

"We tried calling you a couple of times, and I showed up at your apartment, but you didn't answer. I assumed you were busy or working," Keisha told me.

"How long have I been here?" The concept of time was all jumbled in my head. I didn't know if I was coming or going, and it was starting to frustrate me. I needed to get out of there.

"You were brought in two nights ago. We didn't know how to reach your mother, so I said that I was your sister." Keisha walked around the bed and stood on my right. "I was so worried."

"How did you find out I was here?"

She looked at Brett and then back at me, chewing her bottom lip.

My eyes flicked between them both, but neither of them replied.

"Sebastian called me," Brett said a moment later.

My heart thudded against my chest, and a sob escaped my lips.

"Tori, Jose's disappeared."

My stomach dropped. Jose had disappeared? "Why?"

"I don't know. Sebastian was furious," Brett continued.

I took a deep breath. "Jose told me he shot him and that he was dead. Later, before the police came, Sebastian showed up. They fought and…I…don't remember anything else. I remember talking to him on the phone earlier, before I passed out I guess, but I think my head is playing tricks on me. My memories are all over the place."

"Tori, I don't know how to tell you this but…"

I looked at Keisha. She grabbed my hand and squeezed.

Brett took a deep breath. "When he called me, he was freaking out. I've never heard him so upset."

Tears leaked from my eyes, and I squeezed my eyelids shut as Keisha rubbed my hand. I opened my eyes and motioned for him to continue. I know I needed to hear this even if I didn't like the outcome.

"He told me he was going after Jose," he said quietly.

"I know. That's why he showed up. He saved me from getting shot the first time. I remember now. But…that…that didn't last long…though." I winced at the pain in my side.

I turned back to my friends. "Have you heard from Sebastian?" My voice cracked.

Keisha and Brett looked between each other and then back at me, but they didn't answer.

"What?" My heart raced against my chest, threatening to burst if I didn't get answers soon.

Keisha's eyes glazed over. "You…" Her voice cracked. "You don't remember?"

The images from the night played on a loop in my head, but I couldn't remember everything. "I…I remember bits and pieces, but not all of it."

"Tori." Keisha pushed past Brett and grabbed both of my hands.

I looked up into her big green eyes. Sadness and sympathy soared through them. "Keisha, what's going on?"

Tears rolled down her cheeks, making a lump form in my throat.

"Tell me. Please," I begged.

"Sebastian was shot, Tori."

I gasped, clapping a hand over my mouth.

"You don't remember?" Keisha asked me.

I tried to, but I couldn't. "No. But he's fine right? Where is he? I need to see him."

Keisha's shoulders shook.

"Keisha."

She shook her head.

"No…" Tears rolled down my cheeks.

"I'm so sorry." Keisha's eyes were glossy as she looked at me with sympathy.

"After I spoke with Sebastian, he ended up here but he didn't make it. I'm so sorry, baby girl." Brett explained, running a hand over my head.

"Don't, please don't…please. Don't tell me he…oh…I can't. He was…he was alive when…" Sebastian couldn't be dead. He just couldn't. He was the strongest person I knew. Tough and rugged, infuriating, but he was mine. Mine. No, I wouldn't believe it. I couldn't.

"He didn't make it, Tori," she sobbed.

A wail escaped my lips.

"Tori." Brett bent down, wrapping his arms around me.

"I…" Oh God. Sebastian. He was gone. He left me. He actually left me.

"I'm so sorry, baby girl." Brett ran his hand over my head.

"No. I can't handle…" I couldn't breathe. It felt like someone was sitting on my chest. "Sebastian."

The sounds of my screams bounced off the walls, sobs taking over my body. I felt the mattress lower as Keisha lay on the bed beside me, wrapping her arms around me. Sebastian was gone. I would never see him again. Never feel his touch again or hear his deep voice. He wouldn't make me laugh again. He had left me. Jose was still out there, and Sebastian had left me.

Brett headed out a moment later, saying something about needing some air. Keisha continued to hold me as I cried myself to sleep.

CHAPTER TWENTY-SEVEN

A COUPLE OF DAYS later, I was sitting on the edge of the hospital bed with my hands in my lap. It was time for me to go home, but I felt hollow, empty. I didn't want to go home. I didn't want to go anywhere. I wanted Sebastian. Fresh tears welled in my eyes, and I angrily wiped them away.

I was so sick of crying, and I was mad at him. I knew it wasn't his fault, but I was furious that he had left me. Yes, it was irrational of me to feel that way, but at the moment, I couldn't control it.

"Oh God." I rested my head in my hands as my shoulders shook.

"Hey, Tori. You can't get yourself worked up like this."

I looked up into the gentle eyes of my nurse, Beth. "I…I can't deal…"

"Listen." Her eyes softened. "There's someone I want you to talk to." She gave me a card and I nodded.

"Thank you. I don't know if I will, but thanks."

The other woman smiled in understanding. "If you need anything though, you can always call me as well. I…"

I looked up as her breath caught.

"I kind of know what you're going through."

I searched her deep blue eyes and swallowed past the lump in my throat. "I might take you up on that offer. Thank you, Beth," I said quietly.

She smiled and gave me a light hug. I hugged her back as Keisha walked into the room.

"Hey." She smiled slightly.

Beth left a moment later, and I turned to Keisha, sitting back on the bed. "Hi."

"How are you doing?"

I cleared my throat and took some deep breaths. "I…I don't know yet."

She nodded and sat beside me, grabbing my hand. "Tori, I don't even…" Unshed tears filled her eyes.

"Keisha."

"I'm not going to begin to understand what you went through, but just please know that I am here for you now."

I nodded. "I know. Thank you."

She let go of my hand and folded hers in her lap, looking around the room.

"I spoke to my mom."

Her head turned back to look at me. "Oh?"

I sighed. "Yeah, I think I'm going to move back home for a bit."

She let out a deep breath. "Good. I actually was going to suggest that."

"Really?"

"Yeah. I was also going to offer for you to move in with me, but then I remembered…" The thought of Jose finding me was left unsaid.

"I know. Listen, I have something to tell you. I don't know if Brett did already…"

"I know Sebastian showed up at my place while you spent the night there."

"Oh…I'm…" I chewed my bottom lip, trying to not cry at the mention of his name.

"It's fine, Tori. I'm not mad. I knew he had shown up anyway."

My eyes widened and my cheeks heated.

She chuckled. "You guys weren't very quiet."

I laughed, tears filling my eyes, and then fresh sobs replaced my laughter. I missed him so much. The feel of him touching me, his deep smooth voice telling me how much he wanted me, him losing control… Would I ever get over the pain of losing Sebastian?

"Oh, Tori. I'm so sorry, I didn't mean to make you cry. I'm such an ass." She quickly wrapped her arms around me, and I sobbed into the crook of her neck.

"No, it's not your fault." I hiccupped.

Keisha held onto my shoulders and looked down at me. "I'm going to take some time off of work and come stay with you for a bit. Think your mom would mind?"

I wiped under my eyes. "No, not at all."

The phone rang a second later, and I jumped, heart beating against my chest. Looking at the call display, I answered the phone. "Hello, Brett."

Keisha continued packing up my things and I rose from the bed, wincing.

"Are you okay?"

"Oh yeah, just peachy." I rolled my eyes and sniffed, fighting back fresh tears. Let's see how many times we could get Tori to cry in a day.

"I am sorry about everything, Tori."

I sighed. "It's not your fault. Stop apologizing for something you didn't do."

"Well, I should have protected you."

I frowned. "What are you talking…"

"I'm taking you home to your mom's. Is Keisha going too?"

"Yeah."

"Okay, I'll be there in ten minutes." He hung up and I huffed, slamming my phone down on the table in frustration.

Keisha turned to me. "What?"

"Nothing, I'm just…God, I'm sick of fucking crying," I yelled as tears leaked from my eyes and travelled down my cheeks.

She quickly walked to me and grabbed me before I fell to my knees. "Shhh…it's okay. Let it out. It'll take some time for you to not cry so much."

"I just want the pain to stop. I can't deal with this."

"Shh…it doesn't happen that quickly, darling. I'm so sorry. If I could take some of the pain for you, I would."

I cried in her arms as she rocked us back and forth. "I'm so sorry."

"What for?"

"For crying all over your shirt."

She lightly chuckled. "You can cry all over my shirt for as long as you need."

I laughed and then sniffed. "I think I'm going to have to stock up on tissues."

I stood on wobbly legs, and my breath hitched as pain poked me in the side. It wasn't anything too major, but it still throbbed.

"Did the nurse give you anything for the pain?"

"Uh…yeah." I quickly looked away and ran my hands down my face.

"Tori."

"What?" I turned back to Keisha and her eyebrows rose, suspicion written on her face.

My phone rang again, and I grumbled, picking it up. "Brett, seriously, you didn't have to hang up on me."

"Sorry, cochina. It isn't Brett."

I gasped, fingers of fear gripping my spine. "Jose."

"Shit." Keisha swore and went to her purse, grabbed her phone.

"Just because you're leaving the city doesn't mean I won't find you again."

My stomach dropped. "Fuck you, Jose, and don't you ever fuck…"

A deep chuckle came through the phone. "Oh, cochina, I've always loved your candid language, but you really haven't fucking learned anything about me at all, have you?"

I gulped and leaned against the wall, sliding to the floor. "Please, just leave me alone. You got what you wanted. Sebastian is…" I swallowed. "He's dead."

He laughed. "Yes, he is now, isn't he? About time, too. Do you know how it felt to take his life? To watch him die in your arms, knowing that very soon, you'd be mine?"

A sob escaped my lips. "Fuck you, asshole. You got what you wanted, now—"

"No! You listen to me you little bitch, I do not have everything I want. I told you that I want you, so I am going to get you. I am a very determined and very stubborn man. I will have you. And this time, there will be no one to save you. You'll be stuck with me for life."

"Why, why do you want me so bad? I don't understand." Fear burned in the pit of my belly.

"Because I said so! I don't need a reason, do I? But since you're asking, I'll give you one. Now that Sebastian is out of the picture, I still need you for leverage."

I frowned. "Leverage?"

"You'll find out soon enough, cochina. Have fun living with your mom. Remember, I will find you."

I threw the phone across the room and sobbed into my hands, leaning my head against my knees. Arms wrapped around me, and I returned the embrace.

A throat clearing from the door made both of us look up. A large man dressed in a well-tailored suit stood at the door. He was tanned with blond crew-cut hair and bright blue eyes. He looked like he'd just walked off the set of a movie. He was beautiful but not to be taken lightly with dominance and superiority radiating off him.

"Garrith?"

I frowned and turned to Keisha. "This is Garrith?"

Her cheeks turned rosy, and I looked back at Garrith.

"Hello, Keisha." His voice was smooth, lowering when he greeted her.

His deep blue eyes were kind when they flashed back to mine. "Tori, I'm Garrith Jameson. I'm with the FBI."

CHAPTER TWENTY-EIGHT

KEISHA GASPED. "YOU'RE WHAT?"

"Okay…I…"

"You're with the FBI?" her voice rose.

"Keisha." I placed a hand on her arm, but she shrugged it off. She obviously hadn't known about Garrith's job. Seems like they had more secrets between the two of them than Sebastian and I had.

Rising to her full height, she walked up to Garrith and punched him in the stomach.

My eyes widened.

He grunted and grabbed her wrist as she went to punch him again. "Keisha, stop."

"Why didn't you tell me?"

"Keisha, I couldn't."

My head was reeling, and my heart pounded in my ears. "Stop!"

They both turned to me.

"Please, just tell me what the hell is going on."

Garrith turned to Keisha. "You can stay, but you have to keep your mouth shut or else I'm throwing you out."

Keisha's lips tightened, and then a moment later she sighed. "Fine."

He grabbed her arm, spinning her toward him, and whispered something in her ear. Her back went ramrod straight as he pulled her against him. "Garrith," she said breathily.

He let her go a moment later, and sexual tension filled the room as she walked back to my bed.

Walking over to me, she grabbed my hand, helping me to my feet. I looked between the two of them. Garrith was calm and collected, acting like nothing had happened. Clearly they had a thing. How serious it was, I didn't know, but I could see the attraction and the affection they felt for each other. Jealousy curled in my stomach, and I shook away the feeling. I wasn't going to let my unhappiness and misfortune ruin what my friend had.

Keisha and I both sat on the edge of the bed as Garrith pulled up a chair. Her cheeks were flushed, and her hands were shaky. I looked at her curiously, and she slowly shook her head.

"I'll tell you later," she responded.

"I need to tell you some things before I start asking questions," Garrith stated, interrupting my thoughts.

Keisha held onto my hand and squeezed it in reassurance. I swallowed. "Okay."

Garrith seemed to think a moment before continuing. "As you must know already, Jose Alvarez is not someone to be taken lightly."

I scoffed. "That's an understatement if I ever heard one."

He went on, ignoring my commentary. "He's made his name known in the criminal world. At first by dealing drugs, and then he moved on to armory."

"What does that mean?"

"Jose is an arms dealer, and he also…moves things and…is accused of other crimes." He flipped through the folder in his hand. "Among other things, sexual assault being one of them."

I swallowed hard. "Oh…k…"

"Tori, Jose deals guns, ammo, grenades…you name it. He'll get his hands on it and sell it. This is much bigger than some petty drugs," Garrith explained.

I frowned. "Okay. Well…what do you mean that he moves things too?"

"I can't go into too much detail over that, but let's just say, anything that needs to be shipped…doesn't matter if it's overseas…he'll get it there."

"Why are you telling me this?"

Garrith sighed. "With Jose being on the run, we're worried that he'll come after you. With his newfound obsession with you, he won't stop until that happens or worse."

"I think she knows that, ass…"

I tugged on Keisha's hand, interrupting her. "Stop."

Garrith ignored her. "I want to take you into protective custody. With his history of abuse towards women, it wouldn't be wise for you to be alone."

My eyes widened. "What? No. I'm not living that way. I can't…"

"Tori, maybe it's not such a bad idea," Keisha said quietly.

I looked back and forth between the both of them. "No. I'm moving back home with my mom."

"Yes, we know that, and Jose knows that too, doesn't he?" Garrith asked.

"I…how did you know that?"

"Your phone is tapped. We had to bug it to keep an eye on you."

I gasped.

"Just because you're in the hospital doesn't mean that you're safe, Tori. Did you see those big guys walking up and down the hall?"

I nodded, remembering that I had tried speaking to them, but all they did was nod in my direction.

"Those are FBI agents. They're here to protect you, Tori."

"I can't live this way." A lump formed in my throat. I wouldn't live being scared. I needed to leave for good. Maybe moving to my mother's was a bad idea.

"I know, and I'm so sorry but we're doing this to protect you." Garrith sat back in the chair and reached into his jacket, pulling out a small pad and pen.

I sighed.

"I need to ask you some questions."

"Okay."

"It's going to be difficult, but I need you to think real hard for me and tell me everything you know about…" He paused.

I looked up at his hesitation, knowing that he was going to ask me about Sebastian.

"Sebastian Chelios."

"Garrith," Keisha warned.

"No." I turned to Keisha. "It's fine. This has to be done, I guess."

"Hey, you ladies ready?" Brett walked into the room as I was about to ask Garrith to continue.

"Hey, Brett." Garrith stood up and shook hands with him.

"Hey, what's going on?"

Garrith turned back to me. "Brett knows some of what's being going on."

Keisha threw up her hands. "Of course he does. Why does that not surprise me?"

Brett's cheeks reddened. "Oh, I assume you told Keisha you're all FBI and shit?"

"Yeah, I did, and we'll talk later, won't we, Keisha?" He turned to her, his voice lowering, and she looked away.

"Keisha," I whispered.

"I'll tell you later, but let's just say, he's going to fucking hear a piece of my mind. But…" She blushed. "I think I need to dive into that suit first." She said, waggling her eyebrows.

I laughed. "I thought you said he was obnoxious and an ass."

"That's what I thought, but apparently I know nothing about him." The sad look on her face broke my heart, and I turned back to the guys. They were both looking at us with concern, and then Garrith glanced at Keisha, his blue eyes darkening. His gaze quickly flicked back to mine, and he sat again in the seat across from us.

Brett leaned against the bed beside me, placing a hand on my shoulder for support.

"Okay, I'm sorry to do this to you, but I need to ask these questions."

I nodded. "I understand."

"First off, I'm so very sorry for your loss."

I swallowed. "Thank you."

Garrith cleared his throat. "How long did you know Sebastian?"

I thought a moment. Not as long as I wanted to. "Not long. Three months maybe?"

He nodded and wrote something on his pad. "Where did you meet him?"

My cheeks heated at the memory of Sebastian kissing me for the first time in the alley. "At Keisha's job, the little coffee shop."

"What did he tell you about himself?"

I frowned. "Um…not a lot. He was very secretive."

He nodded again and continued to write. "When did you meet Jose?"

I sighed. "I met him a couple of weeks after meeting Sebastian. Keisha and I went out to Brett's club, and he showed up there."

"Both Sebastian and Jose were there?"

"Yes. I was dancing with Sebastian…" My voice cracked, and Garrith looked up.

"Take your time."

I took a deep breath. "I was dancing with him and then he got upset."

"What do you mean?"

"I remember him dragging me through the crowd and we headed for the exit. That's when I saw and met Jose for the first time."

"When did Jose become threatening?"

I cringed. "Well, he looked at me like he wanted to eat me up the very first time I saw him."

Brett's hand tightened on my shoulder.

"Now, I need to ask something, but it might be too personal." He looked up at Brett and Keisha.

"You can ask me with them here. It's fine." I wasn't sure what he wanted to know, but I had no fight left in me, and doing this alone without the support of my friends would have been too difficult.

"Are you sure?"

I nodded.

"Okay." He took another deep breath. "The doctor and nurses won't tell me anything so this is why I need to ask you."

"I understand."

"Did Jose rape you?"

A collective gasp sounded around the room, and I winced as Brett's fingers dug into my shoulders. My heart sped up at the memories of Jose touching me. "No."

"Now I need to ask this also so we can add it to his long list of charges. What did he do to you?" Garrith asked tentatively.

I sighed. "He hurt me and touched me intimately, but he didn't force sex on me. But if he hadn't been interrupted when I was tied to the bed…" Brett growled beside me.

"…he would have. I know deep down that he wouldn't have stopped no matter how many times I said no."

Brett left my side and paced the room.

"Tori," Garrith said.

I kept my eyes downcast and picked at the hem of my shirt. I didn't want to answer any more questions. I wanted to go home and have Sebastian back with me.

"Tori, look at me," he demanded.

Tears pricked at my eyes, and I slowly lifted them, looking into Garrith's deep blue irises. "This is off the record. I promise you, if it's the last thing I do, I'll fucking get him. You hear me?"

I nodded, tears threatening to spill over.

"Now, back to Sebastian." His voice was gruff as he went on. "Do you know any of Sebastian's background?"

I shook my head, my heart heavy that I hardly knew anything about the man I loved. I liked to think that if he had lived, he would finally have shared all of his secrets with me and I with him. Not that I had many, but everyone had their own skeletons. I wanted to tell him mine, and I couldn't.

"Tori?" Garrith's voice was firm, getting my attention again. "It's your stereotypical bad-boy story. He was in foster care for most of his childhood. His mother was a lowlife, father left them when he was young. He ended up falling in with the wrong crowd, got into drugs, fights… He spent most of his young life in and out of jail. He met Jose, and Jose took him under his wing." He looked up at me. "Sebastian wasn't a good guy."

"Garrith," Keisha said from beside me.

"He was good to me," I said quietly. "He loved me. I know he did, and I know that if he could, he would have protected me from Jose but…"

Garrith nodded in understanding. "I know."

I thought a moment. "Can I see him?"

His eyes filled with sympathy, and something else flashed in them quickly before I could tell what it was. "I'm sorry, Tori. The FBI has seized his body."

Tears ran down my cheeks, and I nodded even though I didn't understand. "I didn't even get a chance to say good-bye."

"I'm…"

"He told me he was going to get out," I blurted.

Garrith's eyebrow rose.

"He was going to get out of the lifestyle. I didn't know what the lifestyle was, but I'm not stupid. I knew the business he ran with Jose wasn't legal…but…" I turned to Brett. "Wait…"

Brett's eyes flicked to mine. "Tori."

"Brett has nothing to do with this, Tori."

I looked between them both. "But Jose said…"

"Tori. Brett was working with the FBI trying to bring Jose down."

Keisha and I gasped. "What? I thought…"

"Are you FBI too?" Keisha asked.

Brett laughed. "Fuck no."

"Well, then…"

"Brett was having issues with Jose, and I, being Brett's friend, approached him about a job opportunity," Garrith answered for him.

Brett scoffed. "Job opportunity. Please."

Garrith glared at him.

"What kind of issues were you having?" I asked.

"That's not important." Brett looked away and continued pacing the room.

"So you being an asshole that whole time was all fake, or are you really an asshole?" I couldn't believe what I was hearing.

Brett shrugged. "I can be an asshole, but yes, the whole dinner thing, me setting you up, that was all a lie. I would never do that to you, Tori, but…"

"But what?"

He shook his head, and his shoulders slumped like he was guilty of something, but he didn't answer my question.

Garrith cleared his throat. "What matters now is that you're safe, Tori. It's my job to protect you, but thank you, I've got all the information I need for now." He stood and handed me his card.

I took it and rose from the bed.

"You need anything, you call me. I'm sure we'll be seeing more of each other though." His gaze flicked past me, and I turned to Keisha.

Her cheeks reddened and she looked away.

He cleared his throat. "Anyway, the two FBI agents out in the hall are here to protect you. That's their job. Aside from Brett, Keisha, and your mom, anyone else has to go through them to get to you. All right?"

I nodded.

"Move back home. Take Rooster with you."

Shock tore through me that he knew about my cat. "How did you know…?"

"Tori, we're FBI. We know everything." Humor lit up his blue eyes, and I smiled.

Garrith looked past me at Keisha. "I'll call you."

I turned and saw her biting her lip, her cheeks flushed.

"Oh, fuck it." He walked up to her and grabbed her face in his hands.

My cheeks heated at the intense kiss Garrith left on her lips, and I turned away.

A moan came from the bed, and then a moment later, Garrith walked past me, fire dancing in his eyes.

"No kissing on the job, asshole," Brett admonished.

Garrith gave him the finger and laughed as he left the room.

I turned to Keisha. "Holy hell, what was that?"

"Oh God." She sighed and flopped back on the bed. She then sat up, eyes wide. "Tori, I'm so sorry. I shouldn't be sitting here swooning while you…while you're…oh, shit." Unshed tears filled her eyes, and I quickly walked up to her.

"Keisha, you can't stop living your life just because my life…" I cleared my throat. "…was taken…"

"Shhh…" She wrapped her arms around my neck, and I let the sobs take over…again.

EPILOGUE

A month later…

DEALING WITH SEBASTIAN'S DEATH was harder than I thought it would be. Not being able to give Sebastian a proper burial hurt me. I couldn't say good-bye to him, and I needed that closure. My soul felt like it had been torn in two. I went on with my daily life and took care of Rooster, but a part of me was missing. I felt empty, like a hollow shell that someone else had control over. Like a puppet.

I understood that Sebastian was a criminal and that his body was now FBI property, but I just wished I could have seen him one last time.

Since moving back home, the estranged relationship I had with my mom was slowly mending. But every so often I would wake up screaming at night, my bed soaked from sweat. The nightmares tore at my sanity, and because of Jose, I was afraid that I would never be able to sleep again. My mom would come barreling into my room ready to take on my attacker, even if my attacker was just in my head.

I appreciated it, but even though I was living the dreams, it made my mother's life hell. In the short amount of time I'd stayed with her, bags had taken up permanent residence under her eyes.

I had to leave. I couldn't keep doing this to her, so I started looking for my own place.

Keisha stayed with me until I found a small apartment of my own just down the street from my mother's home. She didn't think it was a good idea for me to live by myself, but I needed a change, and as much as I loved my mom, us living together would eventually destroy our relationship again or harm her health. I had told her that she could visit as much as she wanted and that I was moving out for her.

Keisha would not let me live alone until things with Jose ended, so being headstrong as Keisha was, she up and quit her job in the city and moved in with me.

The two FBI agents, who I now knew as Gordon Cramer and John Lector, were with me constantly. They weren't very social.

I had complained to Garrith, and he told me that they were paid to protect me, not be my friends. I frowned at that but let it go.

After my last conversation with Jose, I hadn't heard from him again. I finally started being able to walk down the street without jumping at every single sound.

I met with the counselor that the nurse, Beth, recommended, and she said that it was normal for a victim of a kidnapping. Beth and I had become very good friends, having both lost a loved one. It seemed to bring us closer together.

Brett visited Keisha and I constantly, even though we both now lived several hours from him. It was nice and a much-needed change to get out of the city, but anxiety still swirled around in my belly. I knew that Jose was out there and that it was only a matter of time before he would find me again.

****

My mind wandered back to the present as I poured myself a glass of water. I went to our balcony and sat on one of the loungers, wrapping my sweater around me.

"Tori, there's mail for you." Keisha came out onto the balcony and handed me a small white envelope.

I turned it over, and the only thing written on it was my name and our address. "There's no return address."

She shrugged and sat beside me. "Open it."

I placed my coffee down and tore into the envelope and pulled out a yellow piece of paper. As I read the words on the page, tears filled my eyes, and I slapped a hand to my mouth. "Oh, God."

Keisha grabbed the paper from my hands as a sob escaped my lips. Her gaze moved quickly across the page and then darted back up to meet mine. "What the fuck is this?"

She handed me back the paper and I read the words again.

Before you, I was blind.
Before you, I was deaf.
Before you, I was mute.
Before you, I was broken.
I was like shattered glass before you came into my life.
You picked up the pieces and slowly put me back together.
You're my glue and you fixed me.
You are and will always be my happy, little one, and I do and will always fucking love you.

~ Sebastian

P.S. Be patient, little one. I will come back to you.

***

I watched as my cochina and her slut of a friend sat on their apartment balcony.

Keisha handed her what looked like an envelope, and when Tori opened it and read what was in the letter, she burst into tears.

God, I fucking loved watching her cry, but being the one to make her cry was way better. The way her tears rolled down her cheeks made me hard.

My dick jumped at the thought of licking the salty beads off her cheeks, and my mind went back to when she was strapped down to my bed.

Shit, if only I hadn't been interrupted. Her hot little pussy would have been tightly wrapped around my cock instead of just my fingers.

I sighed and watched her friend, Keisha, grab the letter out of her hand. A moment later, shock etched her beautiful features. She was gorgeous, but she wasn't my girl.

There seemed to be a change in Tori, but I couldn't quite put my finger on it. My cochina was something else, but I bet that Keisha had some spirit in her too.

I rubbed my jaw as I continued to watch them. Maybe Keisha would come in handy. Two for the price of one, then I could get rid of her asshole brother like I did with Sebastian.

Sebastian.

Just thinking of him set my blood boiling. That fucker ruined everything, and my cochina was going to pay for it. The love she felt for my old partner would die once I got through with her. If she didn't stop loving him and love me instead, I would beat it or fuck it out of her or maybe even both.

She was going to love me. I would make damn sure of it. She had no choice, really. We were meant to be together.

It was only a matter of time before I would reveal myself to her. Let her know that I'd found her. My dick throbbed at the thought of seeing her again, and I couldn't wait.

She would be mine and mine alone. If I couldn't have her, no one could. It would take some time, but Tori and I would be together again.

*****TO BE CONTINUED*****

ABOUT J.M. WALKER

J.M. Walker is an Amazon bestselling author who also hit USA Today with Wanted: An Outlaw Anthology. She loves all things books, pigs and lip gloss. She is happily married to the man who inspires all of her Heroes and continues to make her weak in the knees every single day.

"Above all, be the HEROINE of your own life..." ~ Nora Ephron

Website: http://www.aboutjmwalker.com/
Facebook: https://www.facebook.com/jm.walker.author
Reader Group: https://www.facebook.com/groups/JMsJems/
Twitter: https://twitter.com/jmwlkr
Instagram: https://www.instagram.com/jmwlkr/
Goodreads: https://www.goodreads.com/author/show/5132169.J_M_Walker
BookBub: https://www.bookbub.com/authors/j-m-walker
Amazon: https://tinyurl.com/y7dpjkud
Newsletter: https://tinyurl.com/ya9hycak

Want more? Head on over to my website for my complete backlist!

https://www.aboutjmwalker.com/books

9 780099 383698 5